DIAMONDS THROUGH WATERLOO

RECONNAISSANCE

BOOK 3 in the
Diamonds through Waterloo series

LARRY FORCEY

Typesetting and cover design by Inksnatcher.com

Printed in the United States of America.

Names: Forcey, Larry, author

Title: Reconnaissance/Larry Forcey

Subjects: | BISAC: BIOGRAPHY & AUTOBIOGRAPHY/Baseball Biographies. BIOGRAPHY & AUTOBIOGRAPHY/Biographical Historical Fiction. RELIGION/Christian Historical Fiction.

Description: First edition. | Avak Publishing, 2025. | Summary: "In 1914, two Harvard athletes are thrust from the acclaim of baseball fields to the battlefields of Europe, where duty, desire, and survival pull them in opposite directions." —Provided by publisher.

This is a work of fiction. Many of the characters are historical, and although the events described in the narrative are based on historical events, the interactions with the main characters are the product of the author's imagination. Any further resemblance to actual persons, living or dead, is entirely coincidental.

Identifiers: LCCN 2025910140 | paperback 979-8-9908961-4-7 | hardcover 979-8-9908961-5-4 | e-book 979-8-9908961-6-1

English Scripture quotations are taken from the KING JAMES VERSION (KJV), public domain.

German Scripture quotations are taken from Elberfelder (1871), public domain.

Poem by Ring Lardner (1914) and newspaper article, "Ruth's Run-in With Umpire" (1917), in public domain.

Front cover photograph of Waterloo battlefield by Larry Forcey

For information about special discounts for bulk purchases, please contact the author at larryforcey@gmail.com.

Next to a battle lost, the saddest thing is a battle won.

—Sir Arthur Wellesley

Contents

1914 – Miracle

The face in the mirror was bearable.

Was he really as handsome as she purported?

He placed his right hand on his right cheek, where minutes earlier her left hand had held his head securely while her moist lips introduced him to the magic of intimacy.

"Beware of her," Merlin had warned. "Beware of the Brenda!"

But after what had just happened outside the gate that led to her dormitory on Radcliffe's campus, on that bench far enough away from any lights to give them the privacy needed, Brenda Rey had confessed her attraction to the new star pitcher on the Crimson varsity nine. "You are so cute," she had announced. "You are like Goldilocks."

William had stared back, flattered, yet confused. "Goldilocks?" he echoed.

Brenda had buried her hand in William's thick brown hair. "Uh-huh," she had whispered. "Ever'thing is just right—your skin is not too light, not too dark. Your nose is not too big, not too small, and your hair is not too long, not too short. Ever'thing is just right." And as she finished her analysis, she combed his hair with her fingers, tickling his scalp.

The more she had spoken, the more her eyes had begged, the more paralyzed William had felt. A pain had grown in his head—a sensation that his eyes were on the verge of exploding, his mind unable to grasp what he was supposed to do about this amazingly beautiful woman gazing at him longingly. She had seemed to be waiting for him to do something, but he felt frozen. Her hazel eyes, button nose, flowing auburn hair, and symmetrical freckled patches on each side of her face fascinated him, demanding that he find some way to express his wonder. She clasped his wrist and gently laid it on her breast. Then she'd leaned close, shut her eyes, and pressed her lips onto his. The brush of her hair, the scent of her skin, and the marshmallowy, cushion-like sensation when her lips pressed onto his had created a leap of fire within his chest. He'd felt the urge to wrap his arms around her, pull her closer, press his lips with greater intensity against her. But Brenda had placed his hand back where she appeared to like it best, and as William caught a more acute scent of her hair, he'd felt her lips part, and his wonder heightened.

Those minutes had awakened William. He'd sensed there was more to be experienced, a path that might lead to even more intense emotions. But she had risen from the bench, straightened her hair, and walked toward the gate leading to her dormitory.

"Brenda?" William had whispered.

"Good night, William," she'd said as she opened the gate.

"Can I see you tomorrow?" he had asked, hurrying toward her.

Brenda had closed the gate and without looking back said, "Patience, Goldilocks."

He had clutched the gate's iron bars, watching her walk up the path to her dorm.

Just before entering her building, Brenda had turned, smiled, winked, and licked her lips.

"Beware of the Brenda!" He had thought of Merlin's warning as he watched the door close behind her.

Even seconds after leaving her, on his walk past James Street and back onto campus, Merlin's words haunted him. In the midst of his burning desire to see Brenda again, to be alone with her, he felt that perhaps Merlin was right.

He awoke from his memories and looked down from the mirror.

He felt lost. He felt weak.

He looked back up, hoping to find strength, but instead, looking back at him was a lowly newsboy from the streets of Manhattan. He took a deep breath and looked to the floor, his hands resting on the bureau over which the mirror hung, garnering the willpower to look once more at the mirror, hoping that he might see something to convince him of Brenda's assessment, something that might prove he was worthy of her affection. But instead of focusing on his face, his attention was diverted to the image of his bed in the mirror—in particular, the strange woolen blanket he had inherited from his so-called mother.

He brought it with him to Harvard for many reasons: to remind him from whence he came, to motivate him to rise above his lot, to encourage him to not stop in his search for answers regarding his origins.

The Chalmers family had helped him decipher the writing on the blanket. Uncle Nathan was the one who interpreted the words for him:

The jester's princess chose it,
To manifest her spite.

But what that meant and how it was relevant to the structure, or home, or log cabin that was stitched onto the rest of the blanket, he did not have the slightest inkling.

He lifted his gaze upward, recalling his intent to confirm Brenda's assessment of his pleasant facial features, but again, his mind shuffled to memories of Mr. Chalmers's letter, of the words that had echoed throughout the last five years:

With no basis to determine nationality, with no evidence from whence your ancestors hailed, it was up to me to populate the information on your birth certificate. Although Brother Kemp has informed me that you are a bug of the highest order, I imagine that the following may be hard to digest.

William turned from the mirror, walked to his bed, and moved his hand across the blanket, enjoying the momentary pleasure of the fabric tickling his palm. He then sat, closed his eyes, looked up, and whispered the words Mr. Chalmers warned might be hard to digest:

Your three given names were inspired by the good showing of Keeler, McGraw, and Jennings in the box score from the prior day's game.

Mr. Chalmers was right. William had yet to digest this information. At times he felt honored, at times humiliated, but most times, lost.

The mirror once more caught his attention, and he raised himself from the bed, walked to the bureau, and stared, trying once again to determine the veracity of Brenda's words.

And again, his attention was diverted.

The door opened, and Merlin tossed his satchel onto his bed.

"You gonna introduce me to your new friend?" Merlin asked, pointing at William's image in the mirror. "How long you been standing there like that?"

William did not turn but spoke to Merlin's image. "Do you ever wonder," he began, "how we got here?"

Merlin winced.

"I mean, just a couple years ago—well, really, less than that—we were still kids. Right?"

Merlin walked to his satchel and removed a notepad.

"What's your angle, Ducky?" he asked. "What's going on?"

William turned from the mirror. "I think you were right."

"Right?"

"About Brenda."

"Aah." Merlin nodded. "I see. What happened?"

"It was wonderful!" William felt a large smile on his face when he spoke.

Merlin held up his hand. "Stop!" he shouted, clapping his hands once, then walked up to William and pushed his finger into his chest.

They were about the same height. Perhaps William was a fraction of an inch taller, but whatever height he had on Merlin was far inferior to the strength advantage Merlin stored throughout all the muscle groups in his body. He had been hitting crisp line drives during his freshman year as the starting center fielder on the Crimson nine while William was pitching relief for the freshman squad. In addition, Merlin was the star halfback, setting yardage records during the fall of last season. So even though Merlin only poked a finger into his chest, William felt a force strong enough to unsettle his balance. He took one step back.

"I've told you, Ducky," Merlin continued, not with anger but with a scolding look of disappointment—a look William recalled seeing on the face of Sir Thomas when William did something wrong. "You can't get sidetracked like this. You've got the smarts." Merlin moved his finger from William's chest and prodded William's head. "You can't let things or people like Brenda get in your way."

Silence followed.

Merlin stepped back, studying William as if he was planning some other way of convincing him. "You see the papers this morning? You hear the news?"

William had read the *Globe*'s morning edition. He always did. If he didn't have an early class, he'd spend the morning hours in the library, primarily to catch up on how the Giants had done the previous day. He was still a bit miffed that he was only able to see one of last year's championship games. He was hoping that one of Boston's two teams would make it to the finals this year so he could attend a greater number. But on the 29th of June, the Red Sox were in fourth place, already showing signs of not having what it took to dethrone Mack's mighty Athletics, and the Braves—well, they were horrible as ever, predictably in eighth place, far behind McGraw's Giants.

William was certain it was not the baseball standings that concerned Merlin, but the news in bold print in both the morning and evening editions of *The Boston Globe*: "Austrian Prince and Wife Killed."

"Yes," William answered. "Terrible."

"It's eerie, Ducky. As if you knew something like this would happen. The premise in that paper you wrote—that Napoleon left a mess in Europe, and all the treaties that resulted from it in the last hundred years—one catastrophe is all it will take to light the tinderbox. The dominoes will begin to topple. Right?"

William felt uncomfortable. He wanted to speak with Merlin about Brenda, perhaps get some insight about how to deal with all those crazy foreign feelings he had colliding inside, but Merlin seemed intent on discussing macro events in Europe. Of what concern to Merlin was the micro-agony William felt within his soul?

He was calculating how he might maneuver the topic of discussion back to Brenda when somebody knocked on the door.

William brushed past Merlin to welcome their guest.

"Professor," he exclaimed, seeing his history teacher standing in the dorm hallway. "Come in."

"Thank you, William."

Professor Murchinson removed his hat prior to entering, creating just enough space between him and the doorframe without having to lower his head, then stepped inside.

William shut the door and rushed to his desk, clearing clothes off the chair.

The professor held up his hand. "No need, William. I shan't be long."

Merlin had already moved toward the door and was about to turn the knob to leave when the professor said, "No privacy required, Mr. Jones. Have a seat, please."

"Yes, sir." Merlin turned back and sat on the edge of his bed.

"Mr. Jones. Working hard this summer, yes? We're hoping to witness more greatness in the fall."

Merlin shuffled his legs, shrugged, bit his lip, and looked up at the professor. "We will try, sir."

"Our Ivy League opponents don't know how to handle your speed. On the gridiron or the diamond . . . ehh?"

Merlin squirmed a bit longer, looked to William, looked back at Murchinson, and conceded, "No, sir, I suppose not."

"I am confident you boys are making the most of your time on campus this summer . . . utilizing the athletic fields and equipment. Yes?"

"Yes, sir," William and Merlin answered in unison.

"Very good. You boys make the Crimson proud."

The professor raised his hat to his chest and looked to William, then to his left at Merlin. The congratulatory air with which he spoke disappeared. He seemed lost, struggling to find a way to say what brought him to their dorm room.

"I am certain you've heard the reports?"

Merlin inched forward to the edge of his bed. "We were just discussing it, sir."

Murchinson wrapped his arms across his chest, squashing his hat, seeming oblivious to the damage he might be causing its shape. "It's of course too early to say where all this may lead. We can only hope and pray that the Austrians find ways to punish their neighbor without causing more death. But as you point out in your analysis, William, if one of the major players maneuvers troops against another nation, it will likely trigger the moving pieces created by the alliances that have formed."

The professor paused and, looking down, recognized the punishment he had administered to his hat. For a few moments he maneuvered his fingers over the fabric, attempting to recreate the proper dimples near the hat's center. But he seemed lost in thought, and after one attempt on the right side of the hat, he gave up, looked to the ceiling, raised his hand to his temple, and muttered, "It's hopeless, really. Isn't it?"

Murchinson lifted his hand from his forehead. Several tears crept down the corners of both eyes. William had not seen his professor before with such lack of decorum. He looked to Merlin, and Merlin looked to him.

"I am sorry, boys. I'm afraid this may call for us all . . ."

He took out his handkerchief, blew his nose, then focused his eyes on William.

"Now." He started again. "Several representatives from the campus paper visited me this afternoon to ask my opinion on what might transpire. What all this might mean. Could it blow over? During our discussion, I mentioned the theory promoted by one of my freshman students last spring, and—well, they were fascinated. Wanted to meet him, ask him some questions."

William noticed Merlin nodding, even smiling. Didn't his friend realize the somber nature of what was happening? What did it matter if William's paper was correct in its assertions? Lives had been lost, and if William's theory was correct, many more lives would be lost.

"You can meet in my office tomorrow at noon?" the professor asked.

"Yes," William answered, "of course." And as he said it, he felt the pride that Merlin must be feeling—the pride that caused his friend to nod and smile. And as quickly as the pride came, it was replaced with a surge of anxiety over meeting with upperclassmen, journalism majors who would be asking questions, assuming that William was qualified to answer. But what qualifications would enable him to answer their inquiries? He was only a newsboy from the streets of Manhattan.

"I'll be there, sir."

"Good!" Professor Murchinson seemed to stand a bit taller and clapped his hands once, then said, "Now we can finalize our discussion on the matter we spoke of last week."

"Sir?"

"Regarding my daughter."

Again, William shifted his eyes toward Merlin who was smiling larger, eyes wide.

"She struggled with all her math courses," the professor explained, "particularly geometry. She's been accepted to Radcliffe. Classes start in September. She needs help. Otherwise, I'm afraid she'll get overwhelmed and just give up."

"Yes, sir."

"Good. We'll discuss the time and compensation tomorrow in my office after you speak with the students from the paper."

The professor bowed slightly to Merlin, turned and opened the door, stepped into the hall, and placed his hat back onto his head.

"Good evening, gentlemen," he called out while walking to the stairwell.

William avoided looking at Merlin. The questions and anxiety regarding Brenda battled the questions and anxiety regarding the pending interview with the student newspaper. He could not endure hearing Merlin's voice—asking questions, offering congratulatory words and I-told-you-so's. The voices inside his head were causing enough commotion. The voice which disturbed him most and caused the greatest confusion was trying to convince him how wonderful it would be, what a relief he would feel, if all that had happened between him and Brenda earlier that evening could be forgotten, erased as if it never happened.

Then he could go on with his life.

***

The off-season practices were tedious. Merlin was fortunate to be preoccupied, accumulating yards on the football field while the rest of Harvard's nine were in the gymnasium playing catch, fielding grounders, and hitting softballs against the walls since the weather was not compatible for outside practices until mid-February or early March.

Nonetheless, William was grateful that he had the option to endure the tedium. Last year as a walk-on freshman, his value to the team was not recognized until late in the season. Most of the other pitchers had either proven their worth and been promoted to varsity or had proven their worthlessness and likely would not be on the team the following year.

With just over a month left as a freshman, William had been brought in by the coach during the bottom of the seventh with the bases loaded, no outs, and the game tied. He intentionally threw his first pitch low and inside to a right-handed batter. But he made it straight and threw it with a grunt, though the ball traveled across the plate slower than any other pitch thrown that afternoon. His second pitch started straight, still slow, but curved to the outside corner, making the count even. The third pitch he hoped would retire the batter—a true fastball, on the inside corner, that must have looked so delicious to the hitter as it approached the plate. But the natural tail of William's pitch ran in on the hands, causing the batter to hit a weak grounder to the third baseman, who easily got the force at home. His next pitch to the following hitter was identical in speed and location, creating another grounder, this one to the shortstop—who fielded, stepped on the bag at second, and threw to first for the double play. Four pitches, three outs. In the eighth it took William seven pitches to retire three batters. In the top of the ninth, it took three pitches to retire the side. In the bottom of the ninth, the Crimson freshmen hit three consecutive singles to win the game.

Coach then brought William in earlier with greater frequency and with growing confidence. In the last game of the freshman season, William pitched a three-hit shutout. The following day, word must have reached Coach Mitchell of the Crimson nine— and with the season in hand for Harvard, they decided to start the freshman standout. William gave up one run over seven innings to Dartmouth. As he retired each batter, he thought of Matty's favorite catcher, the one the sportswriters called Chief but whom William called Johnny, thinking that perhaps the hitters he faced may be the next major leaguers to emerge from Harvard's Ivy League rival.

Now as he played soft toss in the gymnasium with one of the Crimson's catchers, he counted the days until early March when the weather may have warmed enough to thaw the fields. Merlin was likely running in the cold, and that fact made William feel a bit more grateful for his predicament. He held the ball in his hand, perusing his teammates, recognizing they were as bored as he.

"Hey, Two-Thirds," Harte, the star catcher, called out. "You going to throw the ball back?"

William grinned. Though he wasn't a fan of the nickname, at least having a nickname implied that the team accepted him. He tossed the ball back to Harte, this time twisting his arm outward, gyrating his wrist just as Matty had taught, creating the fadeaway action. William had held the pitch a secret and had yet to use it in a game.

"What the hell?" Harte shouted as he reached to catch the ball, barely got a glove on it, and cursed more under his breath as the ball ricocheted several yards and he chased it down. "What was that?"

William smiled. "I call it the two-thirds."

"Whatever you call it, keep it under wraps. Use it when it counts."

Harte's commendation was a good sign. He was the leader of the team, the leader on the field. For him to speak so highly of the pitch's effectiveness encouraged William. But the good feeling Harte's words created was erased as the Crimson's star first baseman intercepted William's next toss and told Harte, "Coach wants you to hit some balls."

As Harte jogged to the other end of the gym, William received the first throw from the first baseman. It stung his hand. But he would not grimace.

He casually tossed the ball back.

"Where do we stand, Two-Thirds?" the first baseman asked.

Now he was not amused.

Harte could call him Two-Thirds; that was fine. But not this jerk.

Though the jerk originated the name, when anybody else on the team called it out, William did not mind. Only when the jerk spoke the words did he cringe.

He didn't like the first baseman. He never did, not since the day they met at St. Mary's when George taught the smug school from New York City the humiliation of losing to a bunch of orphans and delinquents.

"I am sorry," Adam Washburn whispered, looking to his left and right. Taking a step closer to William, he said more quietly, "Where do we stand?"

William held the ball. He tossed it up, caught it in his bare hand, and looked up at the ceiling of the gymnasium.

For which of his offenses was the jerk apologizing? For his antics on the Big Field at St. Mary's? For the threat of extortion he made while William worked at the factory of Adam's father? Or for the wise-ass nickname of Two-Thirds, declaring to the whole team that William Jennings was no William Jennings Bryan and would never amount to more than two-thirds of the senator's worth?

"How many times do I have to say it?" Adam pleaded. "You want me to race up to the top step of the bleachers and apologize in front of the entire team? Coach Mitchell included? Listen, we're teammates. We've got to put the past behind us."

William continued to toss the ball in the air, catching it with the same hand from which he tossed it. Then, finally, he let the ball fall into his glove, looked directly at Adam, and waved him closer as he walked to meet him halfway.

William had no intention of accepting Adam's apology. Rather, he would implement a plan using some information he had gleaned through careful research. He would do some extortion of his own. Besides, there was something sinister in all this. Not only was Adam profuse in his apparent regret for past nastiness, but he had taken a keen interest in Merlin—so keen, in fact, that they had almost become inseparable. They took the same classes; both were majoring in economics and business management. Merlin was attending the church Adam attended, a Presbyterian congregation on the other side of the Charles. Adam offered to help Merlin meet business leaders in the Boston financial district; he invited him to Rotary Club meetings and the theater and dinner at some of the nicer restaurants near the college. William acknowledged that much of the suspicion he felt was born from jealousy, but still, he couldn't shake the certainty that this jerk of a first baseman had something up his sleeve.

And that was when he did some digging at the library, discovering that Adam's father had been a silent partner with the owners of the Triangle Shirt Factory where Ruth worked and in which hundreds of female workers met their deaths because of the fire that resulted from unsafe working conditions. Adam had certainly received admission to Harvard prior to his father being linked to the scandal, and this gave William a card with which to play.

"So," William whispered, "rather than me accepting your crocodile apology, I promise not to divulge the scandal in which your father is embroiled. All you have to do is keep your mouth shut about St. Mary's."

***

Merlin was right about Brenda. The day following William's encounter with her on the bench, she was not in her normal seat behind home plate on the Crimson baseball field, applauding and cheering for each of Harvard's nine by name. "Nice turn, Mr. Abbott," she would shout when the Crimson second baseman fielded a double play. "Load the Harte cannon, boys!" she yelled when William's battery mate threw a runner out at second. "Another three-bagger for the express train!" she announced whenever Merlin slid into third after another line drive into the right center field gap.

And just before William would throw his first pitch, she'd scream, "Now pitching for the Crimson: Two-Thirds Jennings!"

And though her absence calmed William, the other players seemed to miss Brenda's support. Abbott let three balls pass under his legs, threw another two over Adam's head at first. Harte's throws to second were bouncing to the shortstop and second basemen instead of popping their mitts. Even Merlin's swings were lame, hitting weak pop-ups and occasional fly balls into the shallow parts of the outfield. But when William took the mound, looking at Brenda's vacant seat, he took a deep breath and smiled, relieved that she was not there, relieved that he felt relief instead of longing. His first pitch popped Harte's mitt with an echo. His smile grew, and his breathing grew deeper. His curves bit with more angle, and the sliding action of his fastballs seemed to awaken Harte, whose throws to second now resumed their normal *pop* upon arrival.

But Brenda was back in her seat the next day and left after practice, laughing, resting her head on the shoulder of a senior Crimson pitcher, holding his hand. Sure, William felt some remorse, recognizing that his teammate was likely to discover much of the wonderful world of Brenda of which William had caught a glimpse, but what he felt most was gratitude that his teammate was absorbing her attention, that Brenda appeared to expect nothing from William.

Even Adam seemed to be happy for William. "You've escaped the net," Adam said after practice one day that week. "There was Carter . . . there was Smith, and White . . . Francis and Connolly. You remember any of them?"

"I don't even know who they are," William answered.

"Exactly!" Adam exclaimed. "Each was a Brenda conquest. Each fell into deep remorse. Could no longer hit a clean liner or make an accurate throw or even field a ball cleanly. She messes with your head. Destroyed them all."

William looked up at Adam in wonder. "And you?"

Adam held out both hands, shook his head, and with somber eyes, confessed, "She's a looker, Jennings. That's true. But there are good girls, and then there are those who are not. If I'm to have godly children . . . must have a godly woman."

William felt the urge to laugh but placed his hand over his mouth, hiding his smile, when he recognized the seriousness with which Adam spoke. Considering all that he had endured at Adam's expense, the thought of his desiring *goodness* felt foreign—two pieces of a puzzle that would never fit.

"We need you, Two-Thirds," Adam concluded. "You've got the smarts," he said, pointing at the top of his own cap, "and you are a good friend to Jonesy."

Perhaps, William imagined, he had judged the Crimson first baseman too harshly.

Sure enough, within two weeks, the senior pitcher had dropped off the team—could no longer find the plate. His pitch selection was not great prior to Brenda's entry into his life. Still, he had lasted three seasons on the squad, and within half a month she destroyed any value his arm held for the team.

"Hello, William," Brenda said the next afternoon, winking as she said it. She climbed to her perch behind home plate and waved at William when he stepped on the mound.

William pretended he did not hear her voice.

"The masterful Two-Thirds Jennings now on the mound!" she shouted several times when William began throwing batting practice. And each time she said it, the volume increased; each time, his pitches grew faster and sharper, and he was able to pinpoint his location with greater accuracy.

"William!" she called out after practice.

He imagined her voice as one of the birds chirping on Harvard's campus. Would he acknowledge a bird? Would he engage in conversation with any of them?

And the more he envisioned Brenda as a bird, the more attention she paid to him, the more creative her cheering became.

"Keep chirping, birdie," the voice in William's head whispered. "But you ain't finding a home in these branches."

Merlin was also correct in his assessment of the accuracy of William's premise regarding the events transpiring across the Atlantic and around the globe. The student paper printed the story about Professor Murchinson's freshman pupil in the first issue of the fall semester. William became a campus icon, stopped by upperclassmen and graduate students who recognized him from the photo next to the published story. They wanted to discuss what he believed would happen next—should the United States offer its assistance?

Despite his popularity on campus, the paper making William out to be prophetic, he'd had no idea that what was transpiring in Europe could happen so swiftly and so horribly.

Each morning he woke while Merlin was still sleeping. Not willing to wait for the campus library to open, he walked to the nearby hotels in Cambridge and purchased a paper from one of the local newsboys, always paying with a dime, waiting for no change, certain that he had helped brighten the lad's morning.

The accelerating catastrophe on the other side of the sea was matched only by the accelerating improvement of one of Boston's two ball clubs. On Saturday, July 18, for sixty-five of the past sixty-six days the Braves had been in last place. Since there were no blue laws in Cincinnati, the Braves played their Sunday game, defeating the Redlegs, 3–2, moving them into seventh place for the first time in over twenty days. The following day in Pittsburgh they defeated the Pirates, moving the Braves into sixth. On Tuesday, the 21st, they shut out Pittsburgh and moved past two teams, now standing in fourth place.

The Braves remained in fourth while the wheels accelerated in Europe. On the 30th the *Globe*'s headline read, "Reserves Called to Colors by Russia." William arrived late to Murchinson's class that day. He had found a newspaper and walked to the Commons, found a bench behind a row of trees, and started turning the pages that narrated the czar's determination to defend Serbia, against whom Austria-Hungary had declared war two days earlier. Another story detailed Germany's determination to ally with Austria-Hungary, declaring an ultimatum to Russia, demanding that they end the mobilization of their troops.

The morning edition on Saturday, August 1, headlined that Germany's kaiser granted a twelve-hour window for the czar to withdraw troops; the evening edition contained stories of Russia's refusal to comply and France's mobilization against Germany. On Sunday, the 2nd, Germany declared war on Russia and threatened Belgium, ordering them to allow access for the German troops to march toward France. The evening edition of Monday's paper announced, "The British Army Will Be Mobilized Tomorrow."

The evening edition of Tuesday's paper announced England's ultimatum to Germany, commanding them to withdraw their troops from Belgium. The Wednesday morning paper announced England's declaration of war against Germany.

Five days later the Boston Braves defeated the Reds at home, rising from fourth place to second place, with only McGraw's team ahead of them. Fifteen days later, on Tuesday, August 25, the Braves defeated the Cubs, moving the Braves into a tie with McGraw's Giants. In just over a month, while the nations of Europe were aligning for war, the Braves had moved from last into first. Within less than a month, fighting had begun on French soil near the town of Verdun, while the Russian Army was attacking the eastern parts of Prussia.

In Philadelphia, on Saturday, September 5, while the Braves were defeating the Phillies and moving into first place again, never to relinquish their lead for the remainder of the season, the Allies abandoned Rheims. Two days earlier the paper announced the German Army was close to Paris. There was a hopeful story, though, on the front page, of British and French aviators scoring decisive victories against the Germans. Merlin asked if he could snip out the story along with the picture of the British flight commander to pin on the wall above the head of his bed. "He reminds me of Ma's brother," he told William. "He's lighter, of course, but the stare in his eyes, the pride—it's the same. He's a pilot, you know, up north in Quebec."

William handed the paper to Merlin along with the scissors he kept in his desk. He had heard the stories of Merlin's uncle, one of the few men with dark skin who was trained to fly. He had taught Merlin the intricacies of a plane's intestines—how to fix a motor, a propeller, a loose wheel. William saw a far-off look in Merlin's eyes as he snipped the picture from the paper, pinned it to the wall, stepped back, folded his arms, and stared at the British pilot—just stared, as if he was formulating something in the deep recesses of his mind.

***

Whatever Merlin was contemplating frightened William. As the days passed in September, Merlin asked William for each of the newspapers he had purchased. He scoured the pages for stories and pictures of Allied aviators, then pinned them onto the wall next to the British commander. As the number of clippings increased, so did the prestige Merlin garnered on the football field. The yards gained against Dartmouth, Yale, Princeton—each game the total climbed. Yet Merlin snipped no clippings from the *Globe* regarding his prowess as the Crimson halfback—only of French and British flying aces.

Meanwhile, as Merlin snipped, clipped, pinned, and daydreamed of whatever he was daydreaming, William was devising a scheme. Somehow, some way, he must attend the Series—all the games in Philadelphia, all the games in Boston. One game last year was not enough.

He had the funds. The proceeds from the one diamond which Uncle Nathan had helped him sell were sufficient to pay for his classes and other expenses in Cambridge. The excess money he placed in two accounts—one at the bank in Manhattan that held the funds earned as a newsboy and the other at a bank in Boston's Copley Square. As a freshman he had an account balance of just over $5,000. He had only withdrawn funds on three occasions—to purchase Christmas gifts for the Chalmers family and twice for textbooks. The account balance had lowered to $4,762. More than enough for Series tickets. Even from the dirty scalpers that robbed desperate fans.

Still, he would need an excuse to skip class.

He knocked on Professor Murchinson's office door, his heart racing. The professor had been so good to him. He even felt that the professor treated him special, as if he were his prized student. He had entrusted him to tutor his daughter Jenny, who was now flourishing at Radcliffe, in part thanks to William's efforts.

"Welcome, Mr. Jennings," Professor Murchinson said as he opened the door. "Have a seat."

William sat in one of the two cushioned chairs opposite Murchinson's desk, the chairs angled in a manner that made the professor's seat the apex in the office.

"What's on your mind?"

William cleared his throat, trying to fight the pounding he felt in his chest. "What you spoke of last week . . . regarding European influence in the early nineteenth century upon life in America . . ."

The professor seemed interested. "Yes?"

"I was wondering . . ." William replied, pondering how to proceed. "I was thinking of your assignment and would like my paper to focus on Napoleon's influence. Particularly with regard to Louisiana."

"I see."

William noticed a peculiar smirk from the professor.

"Well," William continued, "I was wondering, since the original signed document of the purchase is in the capital at the National Archives, could I arrange for a short leave of absence from class?"

The professor straightened his posture and moved his chair closer to the edge of the desk, folded his arms, and turned to look outside his office window, then back at William, his smirk more pronounced.

"I'll make a deal with you, Mr. Jennings."

"A deal, sir?"

"You leave here next Tuesday evening. Take the train, and you'll arrive in DC by—what? Ten o'clock the following morning?"

William shrugged, tilting his head to one side, partly to agree with the professor's time assessment, partly because he was confused as to what the deal might be.

"That gives you almost two full days to study the purchase. I've made arrangements for you with the curator . . ."

William could feel his eyes widen.

"We were classmates back in the nineties," the professor explained. "He will give you full access. Take the notes you need. Take the train back north on Friday, and make sure you get off in Philadelphia . . . Do whatever you need to do there on Friday and Saturday. On Sunday, hop back onto the train. Be back here for class Monday morning. Then around noon, we'll head to Fenway for the game."

Now William felt his mouth gaping.

"We, sir?" William said confused.

"Yes," the professor answered. "You, Mr. Jones . . . Jenny, and myself."

William swallowed. He swallowed again. Nervously. Four tickets? Really? Get four tickets for seats next to each other? Sure, he could purchase four single tickets, but how would he manage four seats together? He knew the professor would want them to sit together, to be able to ask William and Merlin about what was transpiring during the game, garnering insights they might have.

And Jenny was another issue. Who was to sit next to her? William did not consider himself to be a very interesting person, someone with whom a stranger could have an intriguing conversation, but Jenny was in a league of her own, perhaps the most dull, boring person with whom William had ever crossed paths. He had been tutoring her for several months, and only once had she spoken of anything other than the subject in which she was being tutored. She was not ugly, but there was no light in her eyes, no smile. If Brenda was on one side of the personality spectrum, Jenny was far on the other side. William had hesitated from their first meeting to initiate any topic of conversation other than study material. He knew of the professor's family, their tragic history. Jenny's mother had died three years earlier, and with no siblings, just Jenny and her father lived in the large triplex overlooking the Charles.

The one time Jenny did emerge from her dullness was a couple months after he began to tutor her. Up until then, William had always sat at the side of the dinner table, his back toward the living room and its fireplace. On this particular night, Jenny's back was toward the fireplace. As she was working on a theorem, William waited, studying the mantle over the fireplace, his head cupped in his hands. He recognized two firearms from the Civil War era. One, a rifled musket, rested on a hook near the rifle's stock and another near the end of the barrel, its length extending the entire width of the mantle. The second was a double-action Starr revolver, protected in a case situated just under the musket. "Those were Grandpapa's," Jenny had said when she had finished the theorem and noticed William's admiration of the two guns. "Papa says they are representative of our family's greatest legacy—that we invested our lives for the emancipation of those held in chains." William nodded in response and gazed at Jenny, who actually smiled before returning to work on the next theorem.

William wouldn't describe Jenny as homely, for she did have a clear complexion, thick black hair, and a nose and ears that Brenda would describe as Goldilocks-like. Still, the sadness in her eyes, her vacant stare, and sagging shoulders gave off an aura of deep, deep depression. Thinking of attending a World Series with her by his side made William reconsider his scheme.

But there was no turning now. He could not let the professor down. He noticed an eagerness in the professor's expression, reminding him of the little boy in the mirror eleven years earlier when Sir Thomas identified the baseball fanatic in the hotel room.

"Yes, sir. There will be four tickets."

"Excellent!"

***

Since arriving at Harvard, William had been receiving weekly letters from the Chalmers children. David shared what he was learning at school and his plans of training to become the greatest lightweight boxing champion to emerge from the East Side; Naomi and Mara narrated events in the home and their eagerness about summer arriving, when they would again accompany Uncle Nathan to Kentucky, receiving more instruction from their music instructor. Jessie drew pictures of a tree or a swing or a doll or anything that held her interest that day.

During his freshman year, after William returned to Cambridge following the Christmas holiday, the letters continued to be signed by all the children, but only David and Mara would write narratives of their lives. During the spring of 1914, the letters were still being signed by all, accompanied by a drawing from Jessie, but it seemed they had agreed to delegate the composition of the letter to Mara. By the beginning of the fall semester, the letters were written and signed by Mara only.

William wrote short notes in response—classes he was taking, pending tests that loomed. But his schedule was too full to divulge much. He had papers to write, ball practice, and with the arrival of October, a train to catch for DC.

On Tuesday, October 6, William boarded the train for the capital. On Wednesday and Thursday he studied the original document signed by Robert Livingston, James Monroe, and Napoleon Bonaparte, granting the United States over eight hundred thousand square miles of land for $15 million. On Friday, October 9, William boarded the earliest train for Philadelphia and bought a fairly cheap seat in the bleachers at Shibe Park, just in time to see Chief Bender's first pitch of the 1914 World Series.

Bender was getting old. There was no other explanation. He had lost games in the '05 Series because he was pitching against Matty, but now he was losing game one because the Braves were clobbering his fastballs all over the diamond.

Boston scored two in their half of the second, one in the fifth, and three more in the sixth, convincing Mr. Mack to pull Bender out of the game. But it was too late; the Braves had scored seven. The Athletics had only managed one run and four hits against the Braves Dick Rudolph, whose curves were making the American League pennant winners look foolish. Rube Oldring struck out in the third on a pitch over his head. He struck out again in the eighth, swinging at a curve that ended up several feet outside of the plate. Jack Barry struck out in the seventh at a low ball that took so long to arrive at the plate that it appeared Barry finished his swing before the ball arrived in Hank Gowdy's mitt.

Gowdy, Boston's catcher, was the star of the game, hitting a double in the second and a triple in the fifth, walking in the sixth, and reaching on a base hit in the eighth. The Philadelphia fans had given up hope by then, and as Rudolph came to bat in the top of the ninth, they showed their sportsmanship by applauding, and some even standing, to show their appreciation for a well-pitched game.

In the hotel that evening, William purchased a copy of the morning edition of *The Philadelphia Inquirer*, headlined with "King Marches Troops Out of Antwerp; Shells and Bombs Rain on Belgian City." William folded the paper and placed it in his satchel next to the notes he took during his two days at the National Archives.

The next morning the *Inquirer*'s headline read, "Antwerp in Flames as Germany Continues Furious Bombardment." William put down the mug of coffee he was drinking at the hotel's cafe, folded the paper under his arm, walked to his room on the fourth floor, placed the paper in his satchel, sat on his bed, buried his head in his hands, and wept.

Antwerp. Of all the cities in Europe. *Antwerp.*

The only city where he had any certainty his mother had been. It is where she had boarded The *Noordland*, the ship on which William was born.

As the Germans progressed in their endeavors, they were likely destroying any links William had to his past. Perhaps his father had been killed in the siege; perhaps the home of his grandparents was in flames. His body convulsed as his mind replayed the images narrated in the paper. Realizing that his hopes of connecting with his past were vanishing, the curse of his reality grew poignant—his identity as an orphan, a bastard, a two-thirds.

In game two, Boston's Bill James faced the minimum number of Athletics through the first eight innings. Though he had walked the first batter he faced in the bottom of the first, he picked him off before retiring the next two batters on groundouts to the third baseman. Then in the sixth, Wally Schang, the Athletics catcher, hit a ground-rule double into the grandstands but was later caught stealing at third. Then in the seventh, after Eddie Collins got a single with two out, he also was caught stealing, which ended the inning. Eddie Plank, however, was almost as strong, pitching a shutout into the ninth. But Charlie Deal, the Braves third baseman, who had a horrible first game, hitting into three double plays, hit a ringing double with one out, then stole third, scoring on Les Mann's single. The Braves won, 1–0, and went up in the Series, 2–0.

Game three was on Monday, October 12. William had purchased four tickets for fifteen dollars to each of the two games. The professor was a tall man, so William gave him the aisle seat. Jenny sat next to her father, then William, then Merlin.

Before the game began, Professor Murchinson asked William, "Is that Johnny Evers playing second base for our Braves?"

"Yes, sir," William answered, bobbing his head back and forth around Jenny so he could answer his professor eye to eye.

"And that's Home Run Baker?" the professor asked with awe as he pointed to the A's third baseman.

Again, William answered, leaning forward, trying to maintain eye contact with Murchinson.

After five minutes, the professor asked Jenny to switch seats with William.

When Eddie Collins stole second in the top of the first, the professor asked Merlin, "Can you run that fast, Mr. Jones?"

A few more questions to Mr. Jones convinced the professor to ask Jenny to switch seats with Merlin.

The game was back and forth, with Philadelphia scoring one in the first and Boston tying in the second. Both teams scored one run in the fourth. The A's managed three hits up through the ninth, the Braves only two. The game which began with such excitement became a bore. The professor continued asking William a stream of questions while Merlin and Jenny talked.

William tried to multitask—watching the events on the field, listening to the professor's questions with his right ear and to the conversation between Merlin and Jenny with his other. Merlin had not met Jenny until that day, did not even know her name, for William always referred to her as "the professor's daughter." *How then*, William wondered, *had Merlin engaged the professor's daughter in what appeared to be an intriguing discourse?* How had he managed to make her feel so comfortable that she was sharing memories of her mother and stories of her childhood, laughing as Merlin recounted escapades on the streets of Chicago and how he and William had first met?

Furthermore, her eyes were not fixed to the ground. She had brushed her hair away from her eyes and tucked it behind her ears. William could not recall if he had ever seen her smile with such regularity. Add to this that Merlin was not watching the events transpire on the field, even when the Athletics scored two runs in the top of the tenth.

As Philadelphia took their positions in the bottom of the tenth, the starter, Joe Bush, remained on the mound. On his first pitch to Hank Gowdy, the Braves catcher hit the ball so hard that even

Merlin turned to watch it sail far over the center field wall, the deepest part of Fenway. Philadelphia's lead was narrowed to one. The next batter, Josh Devore, an ex-Giant, pinch-hit and struck out. The leadoff man, Herbie Moran, walked, then Johnny Evers hit a soft single into right, allowing Moran the time to reach third. Connolly hit a sacrifice fly to center, and the game was tied.

The eleventh ended quickly—one walk, no hits by either team. Merlin and Jenny had resumed their conversation. Darkness was fast approaching, and William thought home plate umpire, Bill Klem, would call the game a tie, but he let them play on. Philadelphia was held scoreless, and in the bottom of the frame Gowdy came through again, leading the bottom of the twelfth with a ground-rule double into the left field crowd. A pinch runner, Les Mann, replaced Gowdy at second, and Billy Gilbert, another ex-Giant, came in to pinch-hit and was walked intentionally. Herbie Moran bunted, trying to advance the pinch runner to third, but when the pitcher, Bush, picked up the ball, he threw wide of third and the ball raced down the foul line, allowing Mann to trot home with the winning run.

The Braves were up three games to none.

Fenway was not all the Red Sox had lent to the Braves for the Series. The Royal Rooters were serpentining the field, blasting their horns, banging their tambourines, and singing "Tessie" before and after the games.

And this same raucous atmosphere accompanied another strong performance by Rudolph, who pitched another brilliant game on Tuesday, October 13, defeating the Athletics, 3–1, to complete the first sweep in World Series history. The papers the next morning announced the brilliance of the Braves' play—the cunning of Rudolph's pitches, the leadership of Manager Stallings and veteran second baseman, Johnny Evers.

The papers also announced that Germany had forced the Belgian leaders from their country, German submarines had sunk a Russian ship in the Baltic, and Antwerp had fallen.

The clippings over Merlin's bed covered the wall.

And in the evenings, he arrived in their dorm room a bit later.

Most nights, Jenny insisted that she walk across to Harvard's library for tutoring rather than William coming to her home about a mile from campus. After the study session, Merlin would walk her home, often taking detours as far as the Commons on the other side of the river.

Jenny transformed into someone William had never imagined. Somehow, within a few weeks, his perception of her shifted dramatically. Now if someone asked William to describe Jenny Murchinson, he would answer, "Pretty. In fact, Jenny Murchinson is quite beautiful."

And she was happy.

She engaged William in conversation, asking about the team and how he selected his pitches. He didn't feel comfortable going into much depth with her regarding such complex matters, but he would not deny her an answer. "The catcher tells me what to throw. The coach tells the catcher, and the catcher signals to me."

William had known Merlin for eight years. He had always been friendly, always kind, always full of energy. He was still all of these things, but when he was with Jenny, he was even more friendly, more kind, and more energetic.

When Merlin snipped the articles from the paper, pinned them on the wall, and stared at them before going to sleep each night, he was not friendly, not kind, void of energy.

During the first week of November, after the Series had ended, William noticed something else pinned on the wall next to the clippings. It was on a thick piece of paper with fancy writing. It looked familiar, and as he walked closer to get a clearer view, he remembered where he had seen it: in Chicago, at the recital Merlin attended with him using Sir Thomas's ticket.

William unpinned it from the wall and read the names of the composers: Brahms, Sjögren, Rubinstein, Liszt, Sauret, Borowski, and their respective nationalities: German, Swedish, Russian, Hungarian, French, British.

He sighed and shut his eyes, fearing that Merlin's dreams might carry him somewhere across the Atlantic.

1915 – The Rookie

William recognized him at once.

It was the face of a boy who had aged, just as William had aged. But somehow, whenever William thought of his classmates at St. Mary's, he still pictured them as the boys they had been, not as the men they would have become.

He had seen the name in the paper, but it had not registered, not until he sat in his usual seat in the far left corner near the rear of Harvard's library and opened to the page announcing the scores from the games played on Wednesday, June 2.

"Oh, my—!" William almost shouted, and amidst his laugh, he raised both hands to his mouth, remembering he was in the hallowed study ground of the nation's finest students.

But he couldn't help it. His joy at seeing his former classmate on the front of the *Boston Herald*'s sports page had to be shared with someone, albeit that none except William had entered the library on the last Thursday prior to final exams. Only the stern librarian was in the vicinity, and she did not look pleased at William's outburst. William waved at her and smiled, pointing at the paper, as if this might help her understand his enthusiasm. She looked down and resumed her work, shaking her head.

"George," William whispered, "is that really you?" His smile grew and he shook his head. It was undeniable. The picture showed George in his pitching motion, and his left arm in its follow-through had just released the ball. The mitt in George's right hand was nestled to his chest, the tip of the pocket just under his chin. His midsection was still broad, but his legs had lengthened, almost giving his former classmate an appearance of lankiness. But it was his broad nose, his wide face full of eagerness to compete, his eyes armed to the hilt with awareness, his mouth not quite smiling in an attempt to hide his recognition that his talents surpassed all his competitors, yet not quite frowning, revealing his determination to defeat all who dared interfere with his exploits on the field.

On Wednesday the paper announced that George had excelled on the mound and at the plate. He had defeated the Yankees, 7–1, giving up only five hits and striking out four batters. At the plate he was walked twice, and he hit a two-run home run. Enough of a performance to earn him a prominent large picture in the *Herald* with bold capital letters just above it, introducing him to all of Boston: "THIS IS BABE RUTH."

William covered his mouth, laughed more, and gazed with growing joy at George's picture, wondering if he was still the boy who had befriended him, if he still had the knack for getting into mischief, and what his story might be that had led him from the fields, classrooms, and dormitories of St. Mary's to the Boston Red Sox.

William recalled seeing the name "Ruth" in the game summaries, but he never recalled the sportswriters referring to Ruth's first name, other than the occasional "Babe," which William surmised was a nickname only because of the player's youth and rookie status. But *never* had William made the connection, never imagined it was the same George Ruth with whom he had tailored shirts.

In the spring William asked Professor Murchinson if he knew anybody at the *Herald*, somebody that could utilize William's skills in research and writing. Within a week William was offered an internship, serving whatever department needed assistance. As fortune would have it, William was assigned to assist the *Herald*'s sports photographers on most days the Sox were in town. His main responsibility was to juggle two cameras the *Herald*'s photographer brought to the game. As the photographer was taking shots with one camera, William was installing film in the other. The previous year autographic film had been introduced, allowing the photographer to write information on the film he was about to expose so as not to confuse the chronology of events when the film was developed. Within a week of William's internship, the sports photographers had entrusted him with the task of writing the inning number on the film just before handing the unused camera to the photographer.

On Tuesday, June 25, as he wrote "Inning 3" on the autographic film, he heard a familiar sound. George was in the box, with two men on base, and the Yankee hurler, Ray Caldwell, must have left a fat pitch over the heart of the plate because the sound William heard, causing him to look up from the film on which he was writing, took him back to the fields of St. Mary's. It was the crisp, resounding smack, distinctive to the impact of wood on leather that only could be replicated by George himself. The last time

William heard a ball hit with such ferocity was when George salvaged William in the game against the Methodist team. Now the sound was magnified—ten, fifteen, twenty times as loud, and as reckoning—as the ball sailed high, arcing deep into the right center field bleachers, creating a hush amongst the Fenway fans, until a boy in one of the top rows caught the ball. Then the stadium erupted into a chorus of cheers and applause.

George did not have a good day on the mound, giving up five runs and eleven hits, but the Sox still outdueled the Yanks, 9–5.

On the 14th of August, George was pitted against the great Walter Johnson. William had seen this day coming, calculating each team's rotation and schedule, hoping that indeed George would have an opportunity to outduel the best pitcher in the game. George struggled in the third, giving up three runs, but did not allow another Senator to score. Meanwhile, at the plate, he hit in one run in the fifth and had a key hit in the bottom of the eighth, leading to the winning rally that would give George a 4–3 victory over the great Washington hurler.

And then on Tuesday, September 14, against the relentless White Sox, George pitched a two-hit complete game, defeating the hard-hitting Chicagoans, 2–1. He held Eddie Collins, Happy Felsch, Ray Schalk, and Joe Jackson hitless, going a combined 0–13, while he hit a single and double, knocking in one of Boston's two runs.

Each time William saw George step on the slab or dig into the box, he felt a burning, tingling, pounding in his chest. He imagined it must be pride, something family feels for one another when they succeed. But as George's success and popularity increased, William felt a growing reluctance to approach him. Originally, he was hesitant because he would not know how to explain his disappearance from St. Mary's eight years earlier. He wasn't prepared to answer such questions because he still was unsure himself as to the reasons he left. And the prouder he felt of George, the more ashamed he felt of himself. Sure, he was about to begin his third year at the nation's most prominent college. It was true that he had developed into a fine pitcher on the Crimson nine, and yes, he had earned the respect of the scholastic community because of his historical insights on the development of the war and the premise that it was the fault of Napoleon more than any other historical figure for the chaos he introduced into the fabric of European politics. But all of this paled compared to the accomplishments George was amassing at Fenway and at the other seven ballparks throughout the American League.

And, perhaps most importantly, only three people at Harvard knew of William's past: William, Merlin, and Adam. If he were to initiate interaction with George, he feared his secret may be sacrificed.

***

On the morning of Friday, June 18, William was to report early to the *Globe*, for he had multiple assignments. Grantland Rice had asked him to research veteran players in both leagues in preparation for a future editorial, and he was to get this report on Mr. Rice's desk prior to the game at Fenway that afternoon against the visiting St. Louis Browns. So he had no time to linger in Harvard's library. He bought a paper from a newsboy outside the gates of Harvard, reading the paper as he rode on the elevated railway, crossing the Charles to the *Globe*.

The front-page headline read, "French Drive Back Big German Army."

William chuckled, thinking that exactly one hundred years earlier the headline could have read almost the exact opposite: "Prussians Aid Wellington in Driving Back Superior French Forces."

The world was so busy reporting the current conflict, they had forgotten of the historic battle one century earlier on the Belgian farm just south of Waterloo.

William stared out the window. All the people walking, likely oblivious to the impact the French emperor had on their lives, heedless of the opening of the West via the Louisiana Purchase, unaware of the domino effect in Europe which was having escalating impact on America, resulting in calling all its citizens to sacrifice. Today it may be a piece of bread, perhaps some coffee, but tomorrow the sacrifice may become the lives of young men. Some Harvard alumni were training regularly on campus in preparation for entry into the war. Current upperclassmen had also begun training. William was certain that he and Merlin would soon be asked to participate. He thought of Sir Thomas—was he aware of the obsession he had created in William's soul when at bedtime he read him stories of Napoleon?

William looked back at the paper, shaking his head, disapproving that he had lingered too long on the front-page stories. He turned to the sports section and studied the game played yesterday against the Browns. George had performed admirably at the plate, hitting in one run and getting two clean singles, but his pitching was horrible once again—seven runs in seven innings. Still, the Sox held on to beat the lowly Browns, 11–10, moving them into a tie for second place.

The game on Friday proved to be less eventful, the Sox topping the Browns, 3–1. As he returned from the game, opening the door to his room, he was met with a surprise.

Sitting at the desk, next to Merlin, turning pages quickly and furiously through a King James, writing notes onto pieces of paper that would soon join the stack of pages already filled with commentary, was Adam Washburn.

Merlin looked up. "Hello, Ducky."

"Ah, Two-Thirds." Adam turned briefly and nodded a welcome. "Returning home from a long day at the park, eh?"

William would have asked what they were doing, but he had a hunch it had to do with the sermon Merlin was to preach in a couple days at Park Street Church.

"You still coming, Ducky? Yes?" Merlin asked, as he thumbed through more pages.

"I said I would," William answered, hoping not to engage in conversation. "I'll be there."

William had almost come to the point where he no longer questioned Adam's intentions. The arrangement for Merlin to preach was the latest result of Adam's lobbying on Merlin's behalf. It was a bit peculiar to William, considering that someone who had previously expressed no interest in the ministry would desire to stand in front of a mass of people and speak for twenty to thirty minutes, but Merlin seemed enthused, and, if nothing else, his preoccupation with the sermon's preparation seemed to divert his attention from the depressing events in Europe. For two weeks, no additional clippings had been added to the wall.

William looked at his two teammates immersed in their study.

He hung his head, dreading the arrival of Sunday morning. He hadn't been inside a church since he left St. Mary's.

But he had promised Merlin.

***

"Please open your Bibles to the Gospel of John, the sixteenth chapter, thirty-third verse," Merlin requested after ascending the stairs to the pulpit and looking out at the congregation for several seconds. It appeared at first that his friend was frightened. The wide eyes and lost look were things William had never seen before on Merlin's face. But once Merlin invited everyone seated in the pews to open to the morning text, Merlin's words rolled with eloquence.

"John records the words Jesus spoke to his disciples the night before his arrest, assuring them that there was trouble awaiting them in the future. 'These things I have spoken unto you, that in me ye might have peace. In the world ye shall have tribulation: but be of good cheer; I have overcome the world.'"

Merlin paused and looked out across the congregation. He flipped one page of his notes, looked to his left, to his right, then tilted his head upward as if the next words from his mouth would be directed specifically to those seated in the last row of pews. "Our Lord," he said, lifting his arms out toward the congregation, "invites his disciples to join him. But they must face reality. He motivates them to endure the battle by relying on the peace . . ."

Once Merlin spoke the word *battle*, it set in motion a series of images that danced through William's mind—a gifted leader speaking words to motivate his followers, encouraging them to press onward; a leader esteemed and beloved by those beneath him. A leader who promises victory, though death may be the cost. Was this not how Napoleon would have spoken to his troops? Was it not his charisma that emboldened the French Army to brave the Russian winter to capture Moscow? That, following his escape from Elba, convinced the regiment, sent to stop his progress to Paris, to disobey their orders and fall in line behind him?

William woke from his thoughts when he heard a cough. He looked toward the pew just below the pulpit and saw Adam smiling, nodding. Even from William's vantage in the far rear of the church, he could read the pride in Adam's expression.

"Next," Merlin said with no hint of nerves, "I invite you to open to Luke, chapter fourteen, verse thirty-one." William surveyed the pews, noticed people responding to the instruction by thumbing through their Bibles. A young boy and girl seated in his pew, each with a large, leather-bound Bible in their lap, flipped pages, stealing glances at their sibling's progress, then returning their attention to the Bible they held.

After about ten seconds, Merlin looked down and read from the text on the lectern. "'Or what king, going to make war against another king, sitteth not down first, and consulteth whether he be able with ten thousand to meet him that cometh against him with twenty thousand? Or else, while the other is yet a great way off, he sendeth an ambassage, and desireth conditions of peace.'"

Before Merlin finished reading the text, William's mind was set in motion once more.

Planning for battle . . . counseling with generals . . . synchronizing the attack.

Synchronization was Napoleon's genius. He planned and mapped out, using his mathematical wizardry to determine where and when Soult, Ney, and each of his marshals would engage in battle. He used the artillery to pave the way for the cavalry and infantry, usually hours before he planned to send infantry into fighting. Was it any wonder he had been victorious sixty-two times in the seventy-two battles he had led? A winning percentage of .861—greater even than the '06 Cubs! How then could the loss to Wellington be explained? His marshals had cautioned him, warning him that Wellington was not like those whom he previously fought. "Humbug" was Napoleon's response. Had he taken their counsel, would things have ended differently?

A middle-aged man in the aisle across from William raised his arm and wrapped it over his wife's shoulder. He was dressed like he was important—a banker, perhaps. She was dressed in satin and lace, wearing some sort of flowery hat. They looked smug and austere. Obnoxious. Their faces were full of pride, the sort of arrogance that assumes superiority and greater worth than those around them.

"Matthew chapter seven, verses twenty-four through twenty-seven," Merlin announced, helping William restore his focus. He looked to the front of the church as Merlin read:

Therefore whosoever heareth these sayings of mine, and doeth them, I will liken him unto a wise man, which built his house upon a rock. And the rain descended, and the floods came, and the winds blew, and beat upon that house; and it fell not: for it was founded upon a rock. And every one that heareth these sayings of mine, and doeth them not, shall be likened unto a foolish man, which built his house upon the sand: And the rain descended, and the floods came, and the winds blew, and beat upon that house; and it fell: and great was the fall of it.

What if, William thought . . .

What if Wellington had not chosen the high ground overlooking the fields of Waterloo?

What if it had not rained all through the night prior to the battle?

The muddy battlefield negated Napoleon's normally effective artillery barrage. Instead of the balls bouncing and skipping from the ground, gaining speed with each bounce until they ripped gaps through enemy lines, the balls shot from the French cannons sank into the mud, plopping, accomplishing nothing.

"And take comfort," Merlin continued, "in the words we read from First Peter." All in the congregation seemed intent, eager to hear the next words spoken. William looked across at Jenny, seated with her father several rows in front of William. Her posture was more proper than usual, and her head was raised up, not pointed downward or drooping as he usually observed. Professor Murchinson was frequently nodding in response to the words Merlin spoke.

Again, his mind diverted from Merlin's sermon, thinking of the professor and his daughter. Just like last year, Murchinson had asked William if it was possible to get seats for all the games of the Series. He spoke with such eager anticipation, just as he did when he lectured, an intoxicating eagerness that captivated all of his students. William felt honored to be entrusted with the task, so he wrote a letter to BJ, uncertain that he would ever get a reply. Two weeks after he mailed the letter an envelope arrived, guaranteeing four tickets to games at both parks. "And," BJ added to the end of the letter, "the four of you will be sitting with me at the National League park."

William had planned to listen intently to Merlin, but there were too many distractions. Perhaps he was out of practice. Even the two children near William sat quietly, eyes wide, mouths open.

"First Peter, chapter one, verses six through seven," Merlin continued.

The boy and girl looked down and began flipping the pages backward and forward, unable to locate the text before Merlin began to read:

Wherein ye greatly rejoice, though now for a season, if need be, ye are in heaviness through manifold temptations: That the trial of your faith, being much more precious than of gold that perisheth, though it be tried with fire, might be found unto praise and honour and glory at the appearing of Jesus Christ.

Various trials?

Why could he not focus on Merlin's words? Next to the Chalmers family, Merlin was the closest he had to family. Yet once more, William's imagination intercepted the words Merlin spoke and created images of Waterloo that William could not overcome.

The French and British Allied forces were both immersed in loss and death. The rain-soaked fields delayed the start of the battle and caused difficulty for both sides. Napoleon had hoped the sun would dry the mud, but he could wait no longer. At 11:30, he ordered the artillery to commence.

The battlefield had evolved into what Victor Hugo described in *Les Misérables* as a large capital *A*. At the apex of the letter was Wellington's camp, Mont-Saint-Jean, overlooking the rest of the battlefield. At the foot of each of the letter's legs was one of the farmhouses at Waterloo. At the foot of the right leg was Napoleon's base, La Belle Alliance; at the foot of the left leg was Hougoumont, the site of the "battle within the battle."

Wellington stationed over two thousand troops to defend Hougoumont, but in the early morning when the French began offensives against it, Wellington refused to send reinforcements. As the day progressed, the French were unable to take the farmhouse. The closest they got was breaching the northern gate, but they were soon slaughtered by the defending British troops, who killed all the French soldiers that entered the courtyard except a fourteen-year-old drummer boy.

For eight hours Napoleon continued to invest more troops in the seizure of the farmhouse, hoping to force Wellington to divert some of his troops to its defense, but he never did—perhaps, William surmised, a contributing factor to Napoleon's defeat. The very thing he hoped to accomplish against the British at Hougoumont, he committed himself. The loss of troops at Hougoumont, combined with the absence of Marshal Grouchy, who was busy pursuing the Prussians to the east, meant less troops for the frontal attack Napoleon would launch later in the day.

In the afternoon from 3:00 to 6:30, there was a lull in the action—except at the farmhouses. Then somewhere between 6:00 and 6:30, a large blob of black uniforms could be seen approaching from the east. The Prussians had arrived!

***

"And our final passage for the day," Merlin announced, "is from the Old Testament."

William glanced at the two children in his pew. Both were biting their lips, leaning forward.

"It comes from Joshua, chapters seven and eight. I won't read it all. I only want to remind you that because of the sin of one man, Achan, the army under Joshua suffered humiliating defeat against the inhabitants of the city of Ai. Only after the Israelites corporately dealt with this sin did they return to battle. Joshua instructed a portion of the army to lay in ambush behind the city while the rest of the army would be on the offensive to feign another humiliating defeat, thus drawing the fighting men of the city to pursue them in flight. 'And the ambush rose quickly,' we read in chapter eight, verse nineteen, 'and they ran as soon as he had stretched out his hand: and they entered into the city, and took it, and hasted and set the city on fire. And when the men of Ai looked behind them, they saw, and, behold, the smoke of the city ascended up to heaven, and they had no power to flee this way or that way.'"

***

Was Napoleon duped? Like the men of Ai?

William chuckled louder than he'd like. He looked around—all congregants were immersed in the words Merlin was speaking. He looked past Merlin, past the pulpit, and stared into the walls of Park Street, not aware that he was looking into the walls of a church, not aware of the time passing as he considered still more whether Napoleon had blundered at Waterloo. With hesitancy, he blew through his lips, again trying to dismiss the absurdity of the thought—the emperor was no more likely to being fooled than Mugsy McGraw was. It wasn't Napoleon who fell prey to Wellington's cunning, but Marshal Ney!

William cataloged the events as they had transpired: Wellington sees the Prussians arriving from the east; he orders his troops to back up in preparation for their arrival, providing the necessary time to best prepare to utilize a two-frontal attack. Time, perhaps, to communicate tactics with Prussian General Bulow. Meanwhile, Marshal Ney interprets the British troop's backward movement as retreat, thereby ordering a full-out charge of the cavalry. Although

Wellington sees the assault, Napoleon does not—at least, not in time to intervene and stop it. Meanwhile, the British form their squares, the front line of each square bending to their knees, holding bayonets upward. The horses of the French cavalry are spooked, unable to attack with their normal ferocity. The British lines shoot low, aiming at the horses. For two hours the French continue the assault but gain little ground. By 7:30 the British artillery is ripping holes through the French lines, decimating Napoleon's troops, forcing a mass retreat southward.

***

William looked up. The church was empty. The organ had just finished the postlude. He looked behind toward the narthex and saw Merlin shaking hands with congregants, receiving congratulations as they left the building.

Jenny stepped back inside the church, looking at William inquisitively, "You all right?" she whispered.

William raised his hand to his right check and scratched it, grimacing. "Sure."

"Wasn't he amazing?" Jenny almost skipped when she asked. "He was wonderful!"

William followed her into the narthex. A line of twenty, maybe more, were waiting to shake Merlin's hand. All around him William could hear excitement. "What insight," one congregant said.

"Such a good word for us today!" said the woman with the flowery hat.

In the corner of the narthex stood Adam. His eyes were downcast as they focused on the line of congregants waiting to shake Merlin's hand. He was not smiling. With each congratulatory word that was spoken, Adam's face seemed to turn a deeper shade of red, his eyes fixed with a menacing determination.

***

During mid-April seven months earlier, just two days before the regular season began, the Harvard nine were invited to participate in an exhibition against the defending world champion Boston Braves. The game, like the Series against the Athletics, would be played at Fenway instead of at the Braves home park. William was grateful he would not pitch. He was sure to freeze if he were to face Johnny Evers or the Series hero, Hank Gowdy. Still, he had been curious then, as he was now, whether his arsenal of pitches might be as effective against the professionals as it had been against the Ivy League batsmen he competed against. Although the Crimson held an early lead against the Braves, their defense collapsed and fell short, 7–3.

And now in October, although he was in Philadelphia sitting in front-row seats at the first game of the 1915 world championship, and although the team in the gray visiting uniforms was from Boston, neither of the two teams vying for the crown had played in the Series the previous year. Same two cities, two different teams.

He would have liked to see Evers and Gowdy successfully defend their greatness, but they had faltered out of the gates and never showed signs of maintaining the miracle from the previous season. As for Connie Mack's Athletics, the great Mr. Mack seemed to have concluded that his players were past their usefulness, determined instead that they could best be used as commodities, trading them for cash and other players. Eddie Collins and Eddie Murphy ended up in Chicago playing for the White Sox, and Bob Shawkey went to the Yankees. Eddie Plank and Chief Bender crossed over to the Federal League, choosing the higher salary offered by the insurgent organization. Home Run Baker sat out the season, disputing his salary. The most ironic of all the departures was shortstop Jack Barry, who left his position in Philadelphia to defend the other side of the bag at Fenway. As the Series opened one year earlier, Barry was fielding grounders at Philadelphia's Shibe Park for the Athletics. Now at game one of the 1915 Series at Philadelphia's Baker Bowl, he scooped grounders at second base for the Red Sox, preparing to compete against the National League champion Philadelphia Phillies.

William felt a warmth in his bosom. He hadn't recognized its presence until earlier in the season. In the midst of papers, the stress and struggle and anxiety of finding words to write; in the heat of all the battles on the mound, choosing the best pitch in a tight circumstance; in the struggle to resist mounting temptations proposed by Brenda, there was continuous risk. Even when he served as an intern for the *Herald*'s photographer at Fenway or Braves Field, there was the constant threat of making a mistake or causing the photographer whom he served to miss a shot. But when he sat in one of Baker Bowl's wooden seats, something inside him clicked into place, telling him that all was now right and good and at peace. He would look at the players warming up; listen to the coaches shout encouragement or barbs; hear the murmur of fans, the beating of drums, the blaring of horns; detect the aromas of sausages and roasted nuts—all of it was there when he was a bat boy, and all of it was there when he served as an intern. But when he could sit in a seat, a seat all his own for the next one-and-a-half to two hours, this was a kingdom, a palace, a shelter from all the worries outside the park.

BJ had kept his promise. He had secured seats at the National League park and sat with his four guests. Professor Murchinson was seated next to Mr. Johnson, discussing the merits of President Wilson, waving his hands, gesticulating his view of US involvement in the war.

William looked to his right. Merlin was nodding, agreeing with whatever words were coming from Jenny's mouth. Jenny was radiant, dressed in a laced summer gown down to her knees. She resembled the Gibson Girl model William saw in the Macy's window in downtown Manhattan. The more she spoke, the more Merlin nodded and the louder Jenny laughed. She was slapping her knees, brushing her hair behind her ears, leaning forward, and with flamboyant exuberance expressed her enthusiasm as loudly with her arms and hands as with her speech.

Was there any better way to spend an early fall afternoon?

When Pete Alexander stepped to the mound at the start of the game, William felt magic in the air. Fans of Philadelphia had grown accustomed to baseball in October. The Athletics lost the championship to the Giants in '05, then won in 1910, 1911, and again in 1913 before losing to the Braves in '14. But this year it was the Phillies playing for the pride of the city and their awkward star pitcher fighting for their honor. His first pitch was high, and William held his breath, uncertain how the volatility of their ace pitcher might respond. He was fairly certain the fans in the stadium felt as he did. Hooper hit a clean single into center on the next pitch, and Everett Scott bunted him to second, putting a runner in scoring position for Tris Speaker. Alexander walked Speaker, then got Hoblitzell to ground into a fielder's choice, retiring Speaker at second, Hooper advancing to third. Before making one pitch to Duffy Lewis, Alexander shot the ball to first base, picking off Hoblitzell, who was napping off the bag. The side retired.

The second inning, the Sox got one more hit. Again in the third, the fourth, fifth, sixth, seventh—one hit each inning, yet no runs. The Phillies scored one run in their half of the fourth, and as the game headed into the eighth, Alexander appeared in control.

Speaker walked again in the top of the eighth and scored on a single by Duffy Lewis, tying the game. But in the bottom of the inning the Phils added two more runs, taking the lead, 3–1.

Barry started the ninth by striking out. Bill Carrigan sent in Olaf Henriksen, the hero from the 1912 Series, to pinch-hit for his light-hitting catcher, Hick Cady. Although he did not get a base hit, the Phils first baseman, Fred Luderus, booted the ball, and Henriksen was safe at first. Next, Carrigan removed his starter, Ernie Shore, for another pinch hitter.

William felt his heart pound when he recognized George step from the Red Sox dugout, swing his bat, and walk toward the plate.

All George had to do was what he had done all those years at St. Mary's: hit the ball high and far by corkscrewing those hips, extending his arms, flicking his wrists, and meeting the ball on the sweet spot of the bat, just as Brother Matthias had taught all the boys.

William inched to the edge of his seat. George stepped to the plate, dug his feet in the box, tugged the bill of his cap tighter around his eyes, held his bat back from his torso, and waited for the Great Alexander to throw his pitch.

The Philly pitcher read George's enthusiasm perfectly. He pitched just as William would have pitched—a fast one on the hands. George swung, pounding the ball into the dirt, sending a weak grounder to Luderus, who fielded the ball and stepped on the bag for the second out.

Hooper popped out to Luderus to end the game.

The Phillies had taken a 1–0 lead in the Series.

Alexander's pitching performance was the highlight of the game, but it was George's brief plate appearance that excited William. He wondered in which of the next games George would take center stage on the pitching slab.

If George's one-pitch at bat was the greatest moment in game one for William, then the extravaganza prior to the first pitch of game two was by far the most exciting moment of any of the World Series games William had attended.

The game was delayed ten minutes as the crowd and all the dignitaries and players waited for President Wilson and his fiancée to settle into their seats and prepare for a pregame ceremony. A band played Francis Scott Key's "Star Spangled Banner," and William looked curiously at Wilson, then at Professor Murchinson to see if he too noticed that their president had not removed his hat and placed it over his heart. It was not until the final notes were playing that he removed his hat. He seemed so lost in the pomp and excitement of the crowd that he had forgotten decorum. Not something, William imagined, that was a good thing for the leader of their nation.

After the band finished playing, the Phillies starting pitcher, Erskine Mayer, walked to the foot of the stands just underneath the president's seat. The president tossed the ball to Mayer, and plate umpire, Cy Rigler, shouted, "Ball!"

William laughed and applauded with the crowd.

Mayer tossed the ball to his catcher, Ed Burns, who handed the ball back to Rigler. Rigler handed the ball back to the president.

"Thank you, Mr. Umpire!" William heard President Wilson say from the other side of the field. It filled him with a comradery, not only with the president but also with the twenty thousand other fans shouting and applauding their elected leader.

The entire game, William had trouble watching the action on the field. He was constantly looking across at the president and his fiancée, Edith Galt. They seemed to be in love, if that's what love looks like—whispering in one another's ears, laughing, arm resting over the other's shoulder. As William considered this affection between Wilson and his lady, he glanced at Merlin and Jenny. Though they were not sharing any physical exchanges, the interaction between Merlin and Jenny was something akin to what he saw between the president and Miss Galt.

Boston won the game, 2–1, though William could not recall how the runs were scored.

The next two games would be played in Boston. The prior year the Red Sox allowed the Braves to use their stadium to host the home games, primarily because Fenway was a nicer park than Braves Field. But the Red Sox were not so interested in aesthetics. They just wanted to sell as many tickets as possible. So the Braves allowed the Red Sox to host their home games at Braves Field, giving them access to almost twenty thousand seats they wouldn't be able to sell if the games were played at Fenway.

But the games were dreadfully boring. Game three was a repeat of the score in game two—Boston won, 2–1. In the last two games, the Phillies had combined for only two runs and six hits. Early in game three William was missing BJ—not because he enjoyed BJ's company, but because the professor and BJ talked during both of the games at the Baker Bowl. William had all the freedom he desired. Merlin and Jenny were enjoying one another, the professor and BJ were figuring out the world's problems, and William felt no expectation. But now, with BJ absorbed in his responsibilities as the host at the American League park, William was left alone to entertain the professor.

Before the second inning began, William discovered that the best way to avoid further conversations was to inch forward in his seat, place his elbows on his knees, and rest his head in the cup of his hands, his back facing the professor.

"I never knew," he heard the professor mutter. "Hmm . . ."

William looked over his shoulder, hoping the professor was not making an attempt to engage him in conversation.

But the professor was not looking at him. He was not looking at anything in particular. His eyes seemed to be wandering the way William's mind wandered when he was searching his intellect in an attempt to discover a better way of thinking or writing.

"Is it possible?" the professor whispered, biting his lip.

William looked past him to see if Merlin or Jenny knew what might have caused this trance.

William studied Murchinson. No more words were audibly coming from his mouth, but his lips were moving, and William saw perspiration accumulate on his upper lip.

When Boston scored a second run in the bottom of the sixth, the crowd's applause seemed to awaken Murchinson. He looked out toward the field. Duffy Lewis was standing at second.

The professor twisted his head toward the scoreboard, then looked to his right at William. "They scored again?"

William nodded, seeing a worried look in his professor's faraway stare, reminding him of the day he came to his dorm room announcing the assassination of the archduke.

Again, William looked over at Merlin, hoping for some explanation, but he and Jenny were doing their normal thing—talking, smiling, nodding, laughing.

William looked up at the professor.

The professor looked to his left toward Merlin and Jenny, then turned, meeting William's eyes.

He seemed to be pleading, his eyes begging.

He looked down, bit his lip again, and looked away, pressing his eyes, tears creeping down his face.

By the end the game, prior to Boston taking a 3–1 Series lead, William concluded something was terribly wrong.

The professor said he and Jenny would not attend the next games in Philadelphia.

Merlin told William he wouldn't be going either.

Four home runs were hit back in Philadelphia's Baker Bowl. Luderus hit one for the Phils. Duffy Lewis hit one for the Sox, and Harry Hooper hit two. The Sox won the game, 5–4, and the Series, 4–1.

George did not make any more appearances.

The professor grew stranger. More distant. More somber.

Jenny and Merlin no longer took their walks in the Commons.

Merlin focused on football and his studies.

The news clippings above Merlin's bed began to appear again, in greater number, with greater frequency.

1916 – Redemption?

He should be happy. And grateful. Full of vigor and determination.

But he was shaking and couldn't stop the shivering.

Yes, the sky was cloudy and the weather cool. The team had not been able to hold a practice outdoors for most of the winter and early spring. And now here they were at Fenway, scheduled to play against the world champions in one of the Red Sox final exhibition games prior to the start of the regular season. And Coach Mitchell told him just hours earlier that he would be pitching the second half of the game.

Within two hours he would be squaring off against some of the best professional hitters in the nation. Against Hooper and Lewis and Hoblitzell and Gardner. And, if it were not for Speaker's contract dispute resulting in Boston ownership selling him to Cleveland, he'd be pitching to the best hitter, next to Ty Cobb, in all of baseball. And although this was some consolation, rumor was amongst the team that Speaker was at the stadium, planning to watch his old teammates play before he left on a train that evening for Cleveland. Knowing that Tris Speaker would be in the stands analyzing his pitching performance increased the tremors William felt.

But his greatest concern was whether George would recognize him. Would George be brought in to pitch? Would George be brought in to pinch-hit? And it was not what George might *do* on the field that concerned William as much as what he might *say*.

Adam had kept his end of the bargain, and Merlin would never divulge William's past. No other members of the team, no other students at Harvard, not even the professor, were aware of his life at St. Mary's.

It had already been a banner day for the college. Harvard's most prestigious graduate, Colonel Roosevelt, was on campus meeting with the overseers, praising their efforts to train the current students and recent graduates for potential entry into the war. He wanted no fanfare—that's what the papers claimed—wanted to avoid political clamor, stay low-key. Even his sons, Archie and Quentin, both current Harvard undergraduates, were said to have waited outside a home on Beacon Street for their father as he finished a meeting with college dignitaries. But as incognito as the former president was reported to have wanted to remain, the Harvard student body held an impromptu parade for their beloved alumnus, shouting hoorahs and waving hundreds of red bandannas that had become the mascot of his Progressive Party candidacy four years earlier.

The Harvard nine felt it their responsibility to build upon the day's legacy. And William couldn't help but wonder if the team's success would hinge on his performance.

He stared out to the furthest seats in Fenway, to the top row of bleachers rising above the right center field wall, recalling the stadium filled, with no empty seats and little space for the standing-room-only patrons to maneuver for better views. He looked to the far end of the dugout, where he knelt four years ago waiting to pick up the next bat dropped by Snodgrass or Merkle or Chief Meyers or Laughing Larry Doyle. He looked out to the mound, imagining Matty staring out into center field, stunned that Snodgrass had just dropped a routine fly. Then, shifting his gaze to the first base coaching box, he shut his eyes, reliving the horror of Speaker's foul pop falling untouched between Merkle, Meyers, and Matty.

His journey into the past had taken his mind from the present. The shivering had calmed. William closed his eyes, raised his head, relaxed his shoulders, and breathed in the cool New England air. Several minutes earlier he had thrown long toss with the new outfielder, Wyche, whom Coach Mitchell had informed, along with William, that he would likely enter the game in the late innings.

As Percy, the Crimson's right fielder, stepped to the plate, William's shivering resumed its intensity. Within a minute, Boston's Vean Gregg quickly retired Percy on strikes. Seeing his teammate walk back to the bench in failure eased some anxiety, and the shivering again began to subside.

Merlin was up next, and he worked Boston's crafty left-hander for a walk.

Adam followed and in short order walked back to the bench just as Percy had minutes earlier. Once Abbott, the cleanup hitter, struck out, the Crimson nine jumped to their feet and ran out to their positions.

William cringed, remembering how Mahan, the best pitcher on the team, was hit hard by the Braves in the exhibition game

Harvard lost one year earlier. But within five minutes the Harvard nine returned to the dugout, Mahan easily retiring Hooper, Hoblitzell, and Walker. The only mar was a walk to the young second baseman, Everett Scott.

One. Two. Three. The Crimson went down in the second.

One. Two. Three. The Crimson went down in the third.

Mahan walked Agnew, the Red Sox catcher, to begin the bottom of the inning, then easily retired Gregg. *No easy task*, William thought, since the Boston pitcher had hit .350 during their championship season. Hooper got a clean base hit, sending Agnew to third. After Hooper stole second, Scott hit a soft grounder back to the mound. Mahan fielded cleanly and threw a strike back to Harte. Upon receiving the ball from Mahan, Harte began to chase Agnew, who had darted back to third, then threw to the Crimson third baseman, Fripp, to make the tag. But Agnew stopped short of the bag, turned, and darted back toward the plate. Fripp tossed the ball back to home, now covered by Mahan, who caught the ball and cleanly tagged Agnew as he slid into home.

It was played perfectly!

The game remained scoreless.

The Crimson bench stood and cheered, clapped, and shouted encouragement to their teammates on the field.

"Attaboy, Mahan!"

"You the man, Hartey!"

"Nice toss, Frippy!"

William was no longer shivering. He was not conscious of there even being a fear of failure. His only thought and desire was for Mahan to continue his brilliance on the mound, for the other eight players on the field to continue their flawless fielding, and for their offense to somehow find a way to score.

In the top of the fourth, Merlin led off the inning, once more working Gregg for a base on balls, but was caught stealing before Adam hit a weak grounder back to the mound for the second out of the inning. Abbott hit an easy grounder to third, and Larry Gardner uncharacteristically booted it. Then Harte smashed a single, moving Abbott to third. Knowles, the Crimson left fielder, hit a hard grounder toward first. Hoblitzell moved to field the ball, but just before he caught it, the ball hit the bag. Although the Red Sox first baseman cleanly fielded the rebound, Gregg failed to cover first in time to field Hobby's throw, allowing Abbott to score and Harvard to tally the first run of the game.

Mahan retired the Red Sox in order in the bottom of the fourth.

In the fifth, after allowing a leadoff single to Jack Barry, Fripp began a slick double play, throwing to Abbott and Abbott throwing to Adam. Mahan then retired Gregg easily once more.

Coach Mitchell signaled William to begin warming up.

One, two, three, went the Crimson in the sixth.

William trotted to the mound.

During his warm-ups to Harte, he noticed Tris Speaker leaning forward, studying him and smiling, as if William were amusing and entertaining the star outfielder.

He received the ball back from Harte and stepped to the back of the mound, taking more deep breaths, collecting his thoughts, calculating his strategy, wondering if Harte, whom he had always trusted, would be thinking along the same lines as he.

Harte pounded his fist into his mitt. "Let's go, Two-Thirds," he began. "Show them your stuff!"

William started Hooper off with a straight pitch on the inside corner, making no extra effort to throw faster than he had ever thrown previously. Hooper watched the pitch go straight into Harte's mitt, showing no reaction to the umpire's call, "Strike one!"

Hooper dug his right foot into the dirt and held his bat out with his right hand toward William. As William stepped back onto the slab, Hooper shifted his weight back onto his left leg and held the bat back, waiting for William to deliver his next pitch.

"Ain't no way I'm throwing him another straight one," William told himself. And Harte agreed. He held two fingers down, and William threw a high arcing curve on the outside black of the plate. Hooper watched the ball sail into Harte's mitt.

"Strike two!" the umpire announced.

Hooper nodded, then turned his head to spit some tobacco onto the dirt just outside the baseline.

William accepted Harte's choice for the next pitch, glad to see that once again his battery mate held down two fingers and positioned his mitt on the inside of the plate.

Hooper hit the pitch sharply, pulling it down the first base line but directly toward Adam, who fielded it cleanly and trotted to the bag, easily beating the speedy Hooper for the out.

Everett Scott was up next.

As he walked to the plate, a voice shouted from the Red Sox dugout. "Hey, Kid!"

William cringed.

He recognized the voice. It was deeper—older—but the melodic intonation and the rising mimicry were undeniable.

"Hey, Kid!" the voice again called out. "You on the mound—I know you!"

William stepped off the slab and glanced into the third base dugout, fixing his eyes directly onto George, trying to communicate, trying to beg him to stop.

William felt a hand rest on his shoulder.

"You all right, Two-Thirds?"

William turned and looked up at Adam.

"I've got your back," Adam whispered.

William stared at his first baseman. What could he do if George decided to be George and blurt whatever was passing through his mind?

Harte stood from his crouch, removed his mask, and jogged to the mound. "We okay out here, guys? What's going on? You feeling all right, Two-Thirds?"

William looked between his catcher and first baseman, feeling paralyzed.

"Hey," Adam said, "you just retired Harry Hooper!"

This got William's attention, and he looked back up at Adam.

"Your pitch selection was just right," Harte added, "and you executed perfectly!"

William nodded, then grinned at his catcher.

He turned back toward the Red Sox bench. George had moved to the top step and was leaning out, trying, it seemed, to hear the conversation on the mound. But he had stopped shouting, stopped announcing that he knew the kid on the mound, and of even greater promise was the expression of concern William recognized on his face, the look George had worn when William returned from Chicago following Sir Thomas's death.

William nodded. "It's all right," he said softly to Adam and Harte. "We're good here."

He tossed the ball into his mitt, trying to confirm to his two teammates that he was ready to proceed. He nodded once more as both Adam and Harte patted him on the back and jogged back to their positions. William turned and looked out to center field, giving a nod and tip of his cap, trying to communicate to Merlin that he was fine.

Before he stepped back onto the slab, William looked back to the Boston bench, nodded at George, and smiled. He would seek him out later, after the game.

Scott, apparently tired of waiting for William to make his first pitch, swung at William's first offering, a curve on the outside corner. The Red Sox second baseman hit a lazy ball that was slicing toward the right field foul line—easily tracked and caught by Percy.

Hoblitzell watched William's first pitch on the outside corner for a strike, then hit a curve ball into deep center, high and sailing, that Merlin ran down several feet in front of the right center field wall.

In the seventh he retired Shorten, Gardner, and Barry, only surrendering a leadoff single to Speaker's replacement, rookie Tillie Walker. In the eighth he again retired the Sox in order: Agnew, then Henriksen, the pinch hitter who broke New York's heart in 1912, and to end the inning, again forced Hooper to hit an unassisted grounder to Adam. In the ninth he gave up a leadoff single to Everett Scott, but then the game ended on a rhythmic turning double play from Reed, the shortstop, to Abbott at second and on to Adam at first.

Once Adam caught the ball, he held both hands high in the air and charged the mound toward William, who raced and embraced him before the rest of the team joined the celebration.

Harvard's Crimson nine had defeated the world champion Boston Red Sox, 1–0. Mahan and William were the stars of the game, Mahan pitching five innings of scoreless ball and William four. But Merlin had shown his brilliance, garnering praise from sportswriters and Boston's coaching staff. It was not only his defense, chasing down several hard-hit liners, but also his work at the plate. Whereas no other Crimson player reached base more than once, Merlin reached base on all four plate appearances—walking twice, smashing a double in the fifth, and cleanly laying down a bunt in the eighth.

When the infielders arrived, jumping onto William's shoulders, removing his cap, and scuffling his hair, he noticed Adam walk slowly to the dugout, remove his hat, and cross his legs.

William turned, looking for Merlin. But he was on the outskirts of the celebration, outside the perimeter of his jubilant teammates, holding his mitt tight to his chest underneath his crossed arms, looking down at the infield grass of Fenway, shuffling his feet through the thick green blades.

****

Most of the Red Sox players left the field seconds after the game ended. They were scheduled to play one final exhibition the following day against the varsity squad from Boston College, then open the season against Connie Mack's Athletics on Wednesday. George was still perched on the top step, hands on hips, looking at William.

"Can you introduce me?" William heard Merlin ask from behind.

George started to clap. He stepped out from the dugout and walked toward William. "You did well, Kid!" he said amid laughter. "You did well!"

William looked back at Merlin and waved for him to follow as he walked toward the third base dugout.

George walked toward them, and they met just past the third base foul line, in fair territory. "You fellas are a strong bunch," George said, looking at William, then Merlin. "Great fielders, good fundamentals. Excellent pitching."

"I suppose you all had your mind on the start of the season—weren't giving us your best effort—"

William regretted saying it as soon as he spoke the words. But George's smile grew. He clapped his hands with more vigor, moved closer to William and wrapped his arms around him, squeezing him, lifting him in the air, and holding him above his head.

"Look at you, Kid! You haven't changed. Still talking yourself down, downplaying. Still outguessing the hitters, still smarter than anyone on the field."

George set him down, then fixed his eyes on Merlin. "You see what he did to Hooper? Twice even?"

Merlin nodded and smiled.

"He came back to the bench cursing." George laughed. "'What's that kid doing, throwing us looping curves? He think this is the Series?'"

"And you?" George held out his hand toward Merlin. "I suppose you're the Jones we read about in the papers, the Crimson's lightning-quick back—?"

"George," William interrupted, "this is Merlin."

William waved Merlin closer. "Merlin, this is George."

Merlin wrapped both hands around George's right hand and moved it up and down with such energy, William thought he might injure the prized pitcher.

"William has told me the stories . . . of you and Congo and the brothers . . ."

"So?" George turned toward William, while Merlin was still moving George's hand up and down. "He knows?"

William nodded.

"But none of the others?"

"One other," William answered. "The first baseman."

"The tall kid?" George looked up as if trying to remember something.

"He was on the team from the Methodist school we beat with your home run."

George bent down and put his hands on his knees, laughing. "I remember! He was ready to pounce you. I thought he looked familiar. And now you're teammates. Crazy world, ain't it?

"And why the secrecy, Kid? Ashamed? Ashamed of the school? Ashamed of us boys?"

"I'm ashamed of being a bastard, George."

George looked at Merlin with a look of shock.

"What happened to you, Kid? You left Congo and me in the lurch. On the ball field, you were our sure hands at second. You helped us with our studies, even though you were younger. We relied on you. We were friends. No goodbye, no warning. You just disappeared."

William could not answer. He still was not certain how he had concluded it was in his best interest to leave St. Mary's. He still was unsure if it had been wise for him to do so. "I just couldn't stay there with Brother Thomas gone."

George nodded, and sadness in his eyes replaced the joy that had been there moments earlier. "The brothers were good to us, Kid. All of them. You took to Thomas. I attached to Matthias. We still keep in touch. I still ask him for advice, and he tells me that I ought to watch for curves when I'm in the box, stuff like that.

Not sure what I'd have done if he was gone. If I had been in your position, I suppose I may have done the same . . ."

"Brother Matthias?" William said, giggling. "Brother Matthias tells you to watch for curves?"

William looked up at George.

"That's right," George answered, looking irked at whatever William found humorous.

"And still, you don't listen?"

"Kid, when my bat meets a fast one and I hit it just right, just at the same time my wrists twist and my hips cock, and the ball sails . . . there ain't no feeling in the world like it. And I pitch, what? Two, maybe three times a week? I get maybe six or seven at bats each week—at most? You think I'm going to step up to that plate, looking for one of your slow looping curves?"

"But, George," William countered, "you think when you're out on the slab. I've seen you fluster the other hitters. You can do the same in the box."

George smiled, then moved his head from side to side, his smile growing. "Hah!" he said looking at William, then Merlin, then back at William. "If I were on the slab, and up in the box stepped George Ruth, then yes, I'd agree with you. I'd try to outguess the version of myself on the mound. But there ain't no other George in either league, so I will just go on waiting for the straight ones and hitting them as far as I can."

***

It was clear during their first game of the season, against Brown, that their victory over Boston had instilled a level of confidence missing the previous spring. While George and the Red Sox had begun the season with a 4–0 record, by mid-May they had devolved into mediocrity. The Harvard nine, on the other hand, were on a ten-game winning streak.

On Wednesday, May 24, William took a break from life and walked to Fenway to watch George take on the Tigers. He needed the diversion—he was scheduled to pitch the biggest game of the season the following day against Dartmouth, and the day after that he would sit for the last final exam of his junior year, but what made the diversion a necessity was the events that had transpired over the past six weeks.

At Fenway, George performed admirably, giving up only four hits including one to Mr. Cobb, and shutting out the Tigers, moving the Sox one game above the mediocrity mark to a record of 16–15.

The next day it was William's turn to make St. Mary's proud.

Before William stepped on the slab, just after he threw his final warm-up pitch to Harte, he walked one lap around the mound. He looked out into center field, and his heart raged within his chest as he was reminded that Merlin was not there. He looked over toward first, and Adam nodded, pumped his fist into his glove, and set himself into fielding position as if he had nothing to do with Merlin's absence—as if none of what had transpired mattered to him.

Harte signaled for a curve, and though William thought it was a strange way to start the game, he did not shrug him. He obeyed, and when the ball crossed the plate and the ump shouted "Strike," the rhythm began.

As he threw the remaining pitches of the inning, he relived the early days of April, struggling to reconcile his naivete with all that had evolved between Merlin and Adam. He supposed it all started following Merlin's sermon at Park Street. Then, perhaps, the next episode was Merlin's escalating brilliance on the ball field. First, it was his performance against the Sox. Then after the first five games of the season, Coach Mitchell decided to flip Merlin and Adam in the batting order—a decision, it seemed, destined to occur since Merlin was more consistently driving runners across the plate. So efficient was Merlin that often the only opportunity Adam had to drive in a run was Merlin himself, who had just cleared the bases with another of his soaring doubles or triples.

One game prior to Coach Mitchell's announcement, when Merlin was still second in the order and Adam was hitting third, Merlin was standing on the first base bag and received the sign from the third base coach that the hit-and-run was in play. Merlin kicked the dirt once with his right foot, then tapped the bag twice, the indicator to Adam that he received the sign. Adam likewise gave his indicator, stepping from the box and tugging the bill of his helmet. But when the pitch came, Adam did not swing, and Merlin was easily thrown out at second.

The game after Coach made the switch, after Adam hit a triple into right center field, the sign for the squeeze was relayed. Merlin confirmed he would bunt on the next pitch, but Adam tugged at his belt as if he were shaking dirt from his pants—the indicator that he had noticed something between the pitcher and catcher and that he was calling off the squeeze.

As the pitcher made his delivery, Adam sprinted toward home. Merlin must have seen the burst of action from the corner of his eye and squared his bat at the last moment, just before the ball crossed the plate. The play took everyone by surprise, even Coach Mitchell and his coach at third. William saw them look at one another with wide eyes and expressions of anger. Though Merlin made the best of the situation, it was clear to all on the team that Adam had intentionally tried to mislead their best hitter.

***

"Attaboy, Two-Thirds!" Harte's encouraging words woke William from his memories. William became aware that his infield was in the dugout and that his teammates in the outfield had already run past him toward the sidelines. Harte motioned for William to join his teammates on the bench.

The Crimson nine were retired in order.

To begin the second, Harte once more invited William to throw a curve. He did. It was a strike. And again, William searched his memory, wondering how he might have altered the chain of events leading to Merlin's departure . . .

***

Professor Murchinson had eased his restrictions on his daughter. He would allow Jenny to spend time with Merlin only if William was in their company. Although the professor seemed to admire Merlin, William surmised that his mentor did not want his daughter to become romantically attached to a man of Merlin's skin color. Though reluctant, he complied with the professor's wishes for the first couple days, but he had books to read, notes to study, papers to write. He came to conclude his friends needed privacy, so he gave them space.

***

When the umpire shouted, "Strike three," ending the top of the second, William needed no prodding from his catcher to step from the mound and jog to their dugout. Though he couldn't recall the exact sequence that led to the third strike, preoccupied as he was with images of Merlin, Jenny, and the professor, he was conscious enough of his stupor the prior inning and didn't want to cause any concern amongst his teammates.

In the third inning, after the number seven hitter flied out to left, William winced as he received the ball back from his third baseman, imagining what he could have done to prevent the tragic sequence of events, upbraiding himself. He shut his eyes and kicked dirt from the slab, recalling days earlier when he was scheduled to help Jenny study for her final exam in trigonometry . . .

***

While William helped Jenny with a theorem, somebody knocked on the front door. The professor answered, and Jenny, immersed in her studies while facing away from the entrance, did not see her father invite their guest inside.

William shifted his weight in his chair, trying to hide his anxiety when he observed Adam following the professor into the study.

"What?" Jenny whispered, looking at William curiously. "Who is it?"

William shook his head. "It's nothing."

He pointed his hand toward the sheet of paper, inviting her to return to the theorem.

In less than five minutes, the door to the study opened. The professor escorted Adam to the front door, shook his hand, and walked toward the dining table.

"Jennifer," the professor said, his eyes fixed to the floor, "follow me, please."

The professor walked to the study, held the door open for his daughter, and shut it once she had entered.

At first, William could hear only mumbled words. Then there was silence, followed by Jenny saying in a volume William had never heard her speak in previously, "I love him, Papa!"

William felt the urge to rise from his chair, put his ear to the door.

But there was no need.

Jenny's mumbles transformed into shouts.

"He makes me laugh. Makes me think. I come alive. Haven't you seen us together, Papa?"

"I have seen. And I have turned away, wishing I had not seen. This is a nightmare."

"A nightmare! Papa! He has returned me to life. I felt so lost after Mama passed."

"If your mother were here, she would agree. She'd feel as I do. You have disappointed me. You have disappointed her."

William closed his eyes. He lowered his head, shaking it from side to side, then opened his eyes and stared blankly into the dark brown stain of the dining table.

"You will not see . . . ever again . . ." the professor shouted. "You will never spend time with . . . you will never write a letter to Mr. Jones. Ever! Do you understand?"

"I can't, Papa, I can't . . ." Jenny's sobbing made her next words unintelligible.

The study door opened several minutes later as Jenny's sobbing increased in intensity.

"William," the professor instructed, "Jenny's study is done for the evening."

"Yes, sir." William gathered his papers, placed them in his satchel, and followed the professor to the front door.

He had looked up at the professor, hoping to offer some word of encouragement. But his professor's face looked foreign to him with lines of age he had never noticed, eyes filled with rage, and a sagging mouth.

***

The fourth inning started the same as the first three—a first ball curve, followed by an out. When William received the ball back from the shortstop, before he stepped on the slab, the image of abandoned streets of Cambridge settled in his memory . . .

***

It seemed the entire town was under quarantine, studying for exams. The streets were vacant. After leaving the professor's home, William wandered the streets surrounding the campus. He walked across the bridge over which he had strolled with Sir Thomas thirteen years earlier. He thought of how he might narrate the events between Jenny and her father. But when he entered his room, Merlin was not alone. He was seated on the edge of his bed.

Across from him, seated on William's bed, was Brenda.

What was she doing there? They'd all be disciplined if she was discovered in their dorm room—grounds for expulsion.

Even someone as bold as Brenda would not test the resolve of Ivy League bureaucrats. Her presence immediately caused William's knees to buckle.

***

Fifth inning. A curve and a groundout . . . followed by more images and memories.

***

Merlin's eyes were red. Tears glistened on both sides of his face.

William turned to Brenda, noticing that her eyes also were reddened, her face saturated with tears.

As much as he had become frustrated with Brenda's incessant attempts to charm him, and as much as he despised her flirtatious personality, she had become sort of an older sister to Jenny. And Jenny's demeanor somehow had eased the ugly personality traits of Brenda. It was like Brenda had helped Jenny come out of her shell, helped her become more like Brenda. And Jenny had helped Brenda grow more considerate of others. She became more like Jenny.

Yet—what would convince Brenda to return, yea, surpass her former brazenness, cross the street, and enter a dormitory at Harvard?

She was holding a glass-encased box.

William recognized it from the professor's home—the box above the mantle that held the pistol used by the professor's father during the War Between the States.

The glass was broken, and its contents had been removed.

"Jenny is dead," Merlin declared, then broke into tears, burying his head in his hands.

***

Sixth inning . . .

***

William escorted Brenda out of their dormitory and back to Radcliffe. The last thing they needed was to be punished for having a Radcliffe student in their bedroom. He thanked her for the friend she was to Jenny. He had wanted to say something more but just turned and walked back toward Harvard.

Upon arriving back in the dorm, William saw that Merlin had fallen asleep—exhausted, William imagined, from the hours of shock and tears.

When William woke the next morning, Merlin was dressed in his best suit, his suitcase on the floor at the foot of his bed. The newspaper clippings had been removed from the wall.

William glanced at the trash bin, overflowing with the news articles.

He looked to Merlin for explanation.

"I am leaving," he said.

***

Seventh inning . . .

Nobody on the bench was speaking to William.

He looked to his left. Abbott and Fripp were speaking to one another, excited about something, but when Fripp made eye contact with William, he stopped speaking with Abbott and turned his attention back toward the field.

***

Eighth inning . . .

Adam hit a home run.

The team cleared the bench and ran to home plate to congratulate him.

William remained seated. He had no intention to ever acknowledge again the existence of the Harvard nine first baseman.

Harte sat next to William on the bench after returning from the celebration.

"You okay, Two-Thirds?" he asked.

William turned to look at his catcher, realizing that for the first time in that game, somebody on the team had spoken to him. He nodded. "Sure."

Harte did not seem convinced.

"What?" William asked with some frustration. "Of course, I miss Merlin."

Harte stood, looked at William with wonder, shook his head again, and walked away.

***

Ninth inning . . .

Harte asked for a curve.

William thought it odd to start another inning with a curve. But things had gone well in the game up to this point, so regardless of the wisdom of throwing a curve ball to begin all nine innings, he would obey his catcher's suggestion.

The batter popped a high fly into foul territory that Fripp ran down and caught near the third base grandstands.

Wait, William thought. *Has anybody reached base?*

Upon receiving the ball back from Fripp, William turned toward Harte, hoping to confirm that indeed not one player on the Dartmouth team had reached base during the game.

"Keep it going, Two-Thirds," Harte shouted before squatting back behind the plate. "Just two more!"

William turned to face his infielders. None would make eye contact with him. He looked to the outfield, and all three appeared to be studying the batter, intentionally looking past him.

If, as he now suspected, he had not allowed any Dartmouth player to reach base safely, he was certain that his teammates would not want to cross the line of superstition by speaking to him in the midst of the game. He knew he wouldn't if one of the other pitchers on the team were doing what he was now doing.

As he began to turn toward his first baseman to see if he might confirm his suspicion, he thought the better of it, stepped on the slab, and threw three consecutive straight balls, striking out the number eight hitter in the Dartmouth lineup.

The Dartmouth coach sent up a pinch hitter. At least William did not recognize the man stepping to the plate as having stood in the box during the earlier moments of the game.

With the count at three balls and two strikes, William threw a straight pitch, as fast as he could, on the outside black of the plate.

The batter fouled it out of play.

He threw the next pitch, also a straight one, on the inside black.

The batter fouled it onto the other side of the field.

He threw a curve.

The batter fouled it back.

He just needed to retire one more batter.

Coach Mitchell was on the top step, not in his usual spot on one side of the bench. He was biting his lip, clapping like he was a fan. "C'mon Two-Thirds!" he shouted. "You can do this!"

Even the Dartmouth bench was standing—some clapping for their teammate at the plate, some gazing out at William like he was a god, and some biting their lips just like his coach.

William looked in for Harte's next signal.

He held down one finger.

William shook it off, for perhaps the first time during the game.

Harte held down two fingers.

Again, William shook him off.

There was one pitch William knew he had not thrown during the game. He couldn't remember the last time he used it. He hoped he could control it; otherwise, the batter would earn a free pass, and William's perfection would be broken.

Harte held down his hand—balled into a fist.

William nodded. He hoped he'd make Matty proud.

While his right hand was just above his right ear, he turned his hand outward, creating spin. The batter was badly fooled but somehow managed to make contact, hitting a scribbler to the left of the mound, between first base and William.

William darted toward the first base foul line, reached for the spinning ball, fielded it cleanly with his bare hand, and began to make the motion to toss it to his first baseman.

But before he released the ball, another option entered his mind.

He looked at the batter, who had apparently given up hope of reaching the bag before being tossed out. So William placed the ball into his mitt and turned, running toward the first base bag.

His run became a sprint.

His arrival caught the first baseman by surprise.

William stepped on the bag and threw his glove to the ground as he barreled into his first baseman, knocking him onto the infield dirt.

He raised his right hand, and with as much force as he had ever thrown a straight pitch, he impacted the first baseman's face just below his left eye, squaring the side of the nose with enough force to spray blood across the white bag.

The sting in his hand was fierce. He felt he might have damaged nerves or broken a bone, but this fed his rage more. He swung his left fist and did damage to the other side of the first baseman's face.

He heard gasping and screaming from all around and felt someone grab his right shoulder. William turned and pushed away the hand of Dartmouth's first base coach, then shoved him away with enough force to cause him to stumble backward onto his rump.

The body of the first sacker was limp, his eyes shut, his face bludgeoned. William punched Adam's stomach, and the first baseman coughed.

William punched with rapid succession the rib cage on either side of Adam's body, feeling tears begin to well in his eyes.

When Adam's eyes opened, William saw the boy who terrified him on the Big Field at St. Mary's. He saw the arrogant adolescent who threatened him in New York City, the privileged college prick whose antics led to a young woman taking her life and breaking the heart of his best friend.

He lifted his still-numb right fist, swinging it toward the already blood-sprayed face just as Harte arrived, wrapping his arms around William and wrestling him onto the dirt.

***

This was one of his favorite spots on earth.

How often he had wished to walk to this street, turn east, look up, and see the towering bridge like a tree rising from the street's asphalt into the sky. To hear the children playing in the parks and to remember the days he spent sitting on a bench, watching over Eli's younger siblings, making sure they played fairly and were safe, serving as Eli's surrogate while he labored in Panama. More than once he had thought of David and smiled or laughed; more than once had he longed to eat one of the suppers Ruth or Mrs. Chalmers had created, had longed to hear the sweet harmony flowing from the strings of Naomi and Mara's violins. More than any of these, he wished to just sit on the sofa, rest his head on a cushion, look at each of their faces, shut his eyes, and fall asleep.

But the last time he had visited was just after Christmas, before he left to begin Harvard's spring semester. Before he had helped defeat the defending World Series champions, before Jenny had taken her life, and before Merlin had left campus, going directly across the border, not even saying goodbye to his parents. Prior to being expelled from the campus, William had received a letter from his best friend, informing him that he had crossed the border to begin training with the Canadian military in hope of joining the Crown's troops on the Western Front.

How then could he knock on their door, expecting to be welcomed? After all he had squandered?

What was it that Mara had written in the final letter he had received?

William reached into his pocket, opened the envelope, and unfolded the letter. Just seeing the writing gave him a moment of peace. But when the memory of his failures resurfaced, he turned his face away from the letter, feeling unworthy of the words she had written:

Dear William,

I hope you are aware of the joy you bring each of us in our home. Judging by the letters you have written, I fear that perhaps we have not expressed this to you. The words I read often break my heart, when I think that you are the one who wrote them—as if you live in a dark world that none of us could understand.

Do you really believe, as you wrote last fall, "of all that I do, what does it matter? If I graduate, what will that contribute to all the horrible things of which we read in the papers? If I pitch well, how does that help those who are being slaughtered by the Germans? Men, or boys, my age and younger even, are dying in ditches. They rise from a hole in the ground, anticipating their moment of glory, and within seconds their bodies stop working as they are shredded by shrap, or obliterated by bullets, or incinerated by fire, or suffocated with gas . . ."

As I rewrite your words, I weep, William . . . to think that your mind is tortured not just with the events transpiring in Europe, but I fear there is a premise in your life that is far worse. And if there are kind words that we can speak . . . or that I can write that may assuage this premise, I want to know what those words may be."

William folded the letter, placed it carefully back into the envelope, removed the satchel from his shoulder, unzipped the front pocket, and placed the letter inside, patting it twice before swinging the satchel back over his shoulder.

He would not knock on the door.

He turned and walked west.

He could not bear to see their faces, watch their eyes, as he disclosed to them why he was back in the city—why he was not still in Boston finishing his exams, finishing the season with the Harvard nine.

He wandered the streets of the East Side, sitting on park benches, staring across the East River, wondering what he was to do with his life. And, more practically, what was he to do the rest of the day?

Eventually, he wandered to Bialystoker Synagogue, where he had first met Uncle Nathan. He walked down the steps, opened the side door, and walked down the long hall. None of it seemed to have changed over the past ten years. The offices were empty then, as they were now, all except the last office. William stood outside Uncle Nate's windowed door, watching Uncle read a document, considering if he should knock.

Uncle Nathan looked up. His eyes widened. He was surprised, certainly, but he also seemed happy.

William reached to open the door, but Nathan had raced to open it, wrapping his arms around William.

"You have finished?" Uncle Nathan asked, releasing William from his embrace and stepping back, making room for him to enter. "You are one year closer to becoming a Harvard graduate?"

William looked to the ground as he entered the office and then held the arm of the chair closest to the door.

After some silence, William looked up.

Uncle looked confused, studying William. "What happened?" he asked, as he gently moved William closer to the chair and pushed on his shoulder, forcing him to sit, then closed the door and sat behind his desk. He set aside the documents upon which he had been working, rested his folded arms on the desk, and waited.

William tossed in his mind the perspective from which he could present his circumstances, some angle that may rationalize what he had done or soften the blow of Uncle's pending condemnation.

"I was expelled."

Uncle Nathan removed his arms from the desk and placed them somewhere out of sight—probably wringing his hands, practicing the maneuver which he would be sure to use around William's throat in a few short moments.

Still, the expression on his face was not revealing. There was no judgment behind his eyes. *So*, William thought, *it may be safe to reveal more.*

And he did. Beginning with Professor Murchinson, describing Jenny's relationship with Merlin and Adam's interference.

"And when I fielded that soft grounder," William explained, feeling safer with each word he spoke, "I knew the game was done. But before I tossed it to first, I just saw him standing there waiting for me to throw it to him. The look on his face was blank. Absent any notion of the pain he had caused, or worse, happy that it had happened and that he had done what he needed to do to get it done. In a moment I changed my mind, and with all the power in my legs, I ran as fast as I could, making sure I'd beat the batter to the bag . . . I looked to my right, and he had barely stepped from the box when I was a couple yards from recording the final out. I turned to look at Adam, and he was just staring at me with this look of, 'What the hell are you doing?' Before he had a chance to react, I stamped the base, threw away my mitt, and rammed him down into the dirt. Lifted my right hand and . . ."

William stopped. He was not proud of what he had done to Adam's face. Harvard's medical staff said no permanent damage had occurred, but a few inches higher and the punches could have caused blindness.

"I've squandered it all. Everything. All you did for me to get there. All that Mr. Chalmers had done so many years ago. Even my mother, with those diamonds. If it weren't for all that you've done, I would have never had the chance. Now I've thrown it all to the wind."

"Hmm," Uncle Nathan muttered.

"I can't show my face to the family. David, Eli, the girls and Ruth and Mrs. C. None of them."

Uncle was biting his lip. His eyes, normally wandering, fixed on William.

"The former president's boys—Archie and Quentin—you have them in any of your classes? See them around campus?"

"Roosevelt?" William answered, irritated that Uncle seemed to be changing the course of dialogue, a sure sign he had nothing to offer William in moving forward.

"Sure. Archie's a good sort. Never met Quentin."

Uncle nodded, still biting his lip. He seemed hesitant.

"Have I told you how the colonel and I first met?"

William shrugged. "When he was police commissioner, you served under him."

"Before that," Uncle interrupted, "ten years earlier. It was our friendship that convinced me to accept his invitation and join the force."

William shook his head. He straightened his posture, curious and hopeful that somehow Uncle's next words might be helpful.

"He was a newly elected state assemblyman," Uncle explained, "highly capable and respected among the people of the city. He was happily married, expecting his first child. Upon receiving a telegram that his wife had given birth to a healthy girl, he left the state capitol and headed home, learning along the way that his wife had had complications during the delivery. Within hours after his arrival, his mother died of typhoid. Twelve hours later his wife died.

"He walked away from his position, headed west to the Dakotas. That's when I met him. Seeing him struggling to fit in with the frontier . . . just as I had years earlier. I took him under my wing. Well, shoot, we all did. He was such a pugnacious, likable fella . . ."

Uncle's eyes drifted off. William imagined he was immersed with a flood of fond memories. He laughed. Laughed more, then bit his lip and fixed his eyes back on William.

"He returned!" Uncle Nathan said with respect, nodding as he said it, affirming Roosevelt's determination.

"Returned?" William repeated, skeptical of the point he felt Uncle was attempting to make.

"Correct. He returned from the West. Returned to public life. Returned to usefulness. Yes?"

William nodded. "And me?"

"Go," Uncle Nathan said, changing his tone as if he were now a teacher. "Go. Just like the colonel. Find yourself."

"But . . ." William did not want to say the obvious.

"Yes," Uncle encouraged, extending his hand. "Continue."

"Colonel Roosevelt did not slug another human in the face. He was not expelled from Harvard."

"He had nothing to regret? Nothing over which to feel shame? That's what you're saying?"

"Yes, sir."

"We all have regrets, William. All of us. Even Colonel Roosevelt."

William hoped Uncle would continue. He needed something. Anything. Even the past failure of a former president might offer a glimmer of hope for his dark future.

"His despair, his love for his deceased wife . . . his feeling of powerlessness." Uncle Nathan paused. He seemed lost and shook his head. "I can't condemn him, for I've never had a child of my own. But, God grant the colonel mercy . . . He abandoned his daughter, left her in his sister's care."

William nodded. He nodded for the colonel. The colonel, like his mother, must have been under extreme stress and sorrow to have abandoned a child. He nodded for himself, for now he understood what he must do.

The proceeds remaining from the sale of the first diamond his mother left him would be enough to fund the plan formulating in his head.

The colonel headed west. So would William.

The colonel refocused, discovered his purpose by riding horses, herding cows, and living off the land. William would refocus and discover his purpose by traveling the rails, visiting ballparks, and fine-tuning his T-Reports.

***

There were rumors. Rumblings.

In the sports editorials and on the streets of the city, in the grandstands of the Polo Grounds, even at Hilltop Park and the newly built Ebbets Field in Brooklyn, the fans of Greater New York were whispering the inevitable. What they all knew would eventually occur but kept hoping would be delayed one more season: Christy Mathewson's career as a Giant would soon end.

He had given the city seventeen seasons, 372 wins, five league pennants, and one world championship. He was the subject of more than fifty pages William had written—T-Reports comprised of masterful pitching performances, great come-from-behind wins, and strategic pitch selections. But there were other pages regarding topics not related to the play on the field—topics like poker strategy, playing three to four moves ahead of your checkers or chess opponent, umpire appreciation, respect for teammates, kindness, and how to handle tragedy.

On the tragedy page, William was surprised at the long list: McGraw's refusal to play in the championship in '04, Merkle's boner and the one-game playoff loss to the Cubs in '08, Baker's home runs and loss to the Athletics in '11, the 1912 fiascos including Snodgrass's drop and Speaker's foul pop dropping between Meyers, Merkle, and Matty. The loss in '13, the loss of his younger brother.

Still, there was nobody on the team, nobody in either league, whom William believed to be more reliable on the mound, more dominant, more cunning. With each defeat, with each setback and heartache, still he excelled, thrived, and improved. Still, he was kind, respectful, and friendly. Still, he was Matty.

Now after seventeen years of dominance, he was used mostly in relief and had only won three games all season. The year following their defeat by the Athletics, he had won twenty-four games, his ERA rising to a mediocre 3.00. The next year his record fell to 8–14, and his ERA continued to climb upward to a pedestrian 3.58. William had witnessed the friendship between Matty and

McGraw, and he had firsthand knowledge of McGraw's thirst for victory. Which of these two loyalties would convince McGraw to take action?

Uncle Nathan provided William with a room in the apartment building where he lived and served as landlord. In exchange, William assisted Uncle with his photography clients. In particular, Uncle had been commissioned by the New York City Council to provide a comprehensive catalog of the tenements on the Lower East Side. Previously, they had relied on Jacob Riis to provide the photographs, but he had passed two years earlier, and now they relied on Riis's disciples. The fact that Uncle Nathan, who had worked closer with Riis than any of his other associates, had entrusted William with the task helped ease the regret and shame over the events at Harvard that William replayed daily in his mind.

Early each morning he would wake and receive a list of addresses from Uncle, along with a letter he had signed authorizing William access to most of the tenement roofs on the Lower East Side. Once atop the roofs, he would set the box camera onto the tripod and spend one to two hours photographing the city's tenements. By noon he'd have visited two or three roofs. He'd race the equipment back to Uncle's basement, hurry to the nearest train station, and catch an afternoon game at the Polo Grounds, Hilltop, or Ebbets.

He went to the game against Cincinnati on June 2, saw Matty get pulled in the third by McGraw after he had already surrendered three runs to what most considered to be the worst lineup in the National League. On June 14, although he pitched a complete game, he lost, giving up four unearned runs to the Cubs. On the 21st he entered the game in relief, losing to the Braves. On the 22nd, though Matty did not enter the game, the Giants lost in eleven innings. The highlight occurred in the top of the eleventh when Johnny Evers, shuffling from third base, started for home, catching the Giants young righty, Rube Schauer, napping, and led his teammates to the first triple steal of the season.

On the 24th and the 26th, William followed the team to Brooklyn, making his first visit to the new stadium across the East River. Matty pitched in relief both games, giving up only one run in six innings and notching a win. William almost missed the victory as he wandered the corridors of Ebbets, catching the sight lines from the first base and third base stands. He looked up with wonder at the chandelier in the rotunda, the light fixture held by a large chain and comprised of twelve arms, shaped as bats, sprouting from its center, each bat holding at its end an electrically illuminated lamp shaped as a baseball.

On the Fourth of July, as rumors escalated of a pending Matty trade, William caught both games of the Giants doubleheader against the visiting Robins of Brooklyn. Matty pitched six and two-thirds innings of relief, losing his fourth game of the season.

It was his last appearance as a Giant. Two weeks later McGraw traded him, along with teammates Edd Roush and Bill McKechnie, to the Reds for Buck Herzog and Red Killefer.

The city's heart was broken. William felt torn. He was sad to see Matty leave, but he was happy for the opportunity it presented his hero. McGraw packaged the deal so that Matty would be the new manager for the Cincinnati club. The Reds were in last place with a record of 35–50. Their best player, Hal Chase, was a magnificent hitter and slick fielder, one of the best players in either league. But there had always been rumors circulating about Chase's integrity, his taste for living large and making blunders on the field when cash on hand was short. William cringed, thinking of the pending conflict that likely would emerge between the Reds star first baseman and the team's new manager.

Matty had left town to head west. William figured it was time for him to embark on his journey.

As soon as news of Matty's trade hit the papers, William spoke with Uncle Nathan, assuring him that all the photographs from all the rooftops he had requested were developed and on his worktable in the basement. Upon dismissal from his duties, William packed his satchel and caught the southbound train for DC. He arrived in time to watch the last seven innings of the White Sox defeating the Senators. He stayed in the capital one more day before departing for Pittsburgh, where he watched the Pirates play the visiting Phillies. From Pittsburgh he traveled north to Cleveland in the midst of a four-game set against the Red Sox. He had dinner with George after the game on Thursday and after Friday's game boarded the train with him for Detroit. On the 31st George pitched a three-hit shutout, defeating Cobb and his teammates. Of particular interest for William was Detroit's losing pitcher, Harry Coveleski, the pesky Polack who dashed the Giants' hopes back in '08 when he was a member of the Phillies. During the game William reached into his satchel, searching for his T-Report on Coveleski, and added the following notes when the pitcher was pulled from the game in the fifth inning:

"Commendable. Resilient. Still throwing effectively. ERA slightly higher than 2.00 . . . If it hadn't been for the poor defense behind him, he'd still be in the game, pitching a shutout. If it weren't George pitching on the other side, I'd be a little sad."

After Detroit, he boarded the train for Chicago and watched the Athletics get humiliated by the White Sox. From Chicago he went to St. Louis, reuniting with George as the Sox played the Browns. Then he headed back east to Philadelphia, north to Manhattan, and on the 15th of August he traveled north to Boston, hoping to witness the second matchup of George against the great Walter Johnson. George had defeated the Big Train back on June 1, pitching a three-hit shutout. Two-and-a-half months later George would defeat him again, pitching an eight-hit shutout. By this time the Sox had risen from mediocrity and were leading the league in wins. As William traveled back west to Pittsburgh, then Cincinnati, he lingered two weeks, traveling between the two rivals, hoping to catch Matty pitching one last time.

As the end of August approached, a new rumor began to circulate that Matty would pitch one game for the Reds against his old rivals, Mordecai Brown and the Chicago Cubs. William adjusted the next week of his itinerary to ensure he would be in Chicago. On Monday, September 4, Matty defeated Three Finger Brown, giving up eight runs and fifteen hits—the ugliest-looking win of his career. And his last.

After the game, the Red Sox and Braves were each atop the standings—providing what potentially could be the second time two teams from the same city competed for the world championship, creating excitement and nostalgia and sadness as William recalled the '06 Series between the two clubs in Chicago. But upon William's return to New York at the end of September, it was clear that the Red Sox would have an opportunity to defend the championship from the prior season. The Braves, however, had faltered, and in their place the Robins had risen to prominence.

"The Robins in the Series?" Eli muttered one afternoon when they met at Ebbets.

Uncle Nathan had arranged for Eli to attend a game with the two of them. William had expressed his shame and hesitancy over what the Chalmers family may think of him and figured Uncle had made this arrangement with Eli to perhaps ease a transition back into their presence.

William was grateful and hopeful that Uncle was right.

"Papa would be giddy," Eli said with excitement. "He'd be chomping. Unable to wait. They had been so awful for so long. Now they have a chance to win the title!"

"And we will be there." William held up a set of red tickets for the games in Boston in his left hand and a set of blue tickets in his right hand for the games to be played in Brooklyn.

***

Before one pitch had been thrown in the 1916 World Series, William was disappointed. There had been speculation amongst the leading sportswriters that Boston's robust Rube would pitch the opening game. After all, George had won twenty-three games, pitched a league-leading nine shutouts, and finished the season with an ERA well below the 2.00 mark, by far the best statistics on the Boston staff. But Carrigan decided to entrust the first game to veteran Ernie Shore.

To accommodate the demand for tickets, the Red Sox ownership requested the use of Braves Field again. The mood was somber. It was as though Bostonians had grown so accustomed to baseball in October that they were conserving energy.

Brooklyn was a young team, sprinkled with veterans, some of whom William knew well—Chief Meyers behind the plate, Rube Marquad, and Fred Merkle. Their high-powered offense, led by Zack Wheat and high-strung Casey Stengel, kept the team at the top of the standings for most of the season. They were led by another of McGraw's old cronies, Wilbert Robinson, beloved by the fans and the organization so much that they adopted part of Rotund Robbie's last name as their team name—the Robins.

"Do they have a chance?" Eli asked, once Shore struck out Jake Daubert on three pitches for the second out of the inning.

A late rally still fell short, with Brooklyn losing the opening game, 6–5.

"Why?" Eli asked. "Why did they have to get our hopes up like that?"

The sky had been clear for the first game, but the weather was cool. At the start of game two, the sky was clearer, the sun brighter, and the weather warmer. The only discomfort in the air was a slight breeze that blew into the fans who sat on the first base side of the stadium. What could be a mild irritant for the fans could be a welcomed ally for the pitchers. The deep center field wall, standing ten feet high, was 505 feet from home plate, creating cavernous alleys in which balls fell untouched, rolling to the fence. By the time the outfielder picked up the ball, the batter was nearing third base or making his way toward home. William raised his head, feeling the wind tussle his hair, certain that George would utilize the wind to his advantage, certain that he would rely on his straight pitch more than normal since the wind would impede hard-hit balls.

"Did you ever think he was this good?" Eli asked William as George jogged to the mound, picked up the ball at the edge of the grass, and threw his first warm-up toss to Pinch Thomas.

"He was better than any of us," William answered, "but we didn't get out much. How could we know?"

Rotund Robbie shuffled his lineup, moving Hi Myers from the leadoff to the number three hitter. George worked Brooklyn's leadoff man, Jimmy Johnston, to a full count before he hit a fly out to Tillie Walker in center. Daubert hit a high pop into foul territory that was chased down and caught by Larry Gardner. George's first pitch to Myers was wide, but his next one was straight, splitting the plate. Myers belted it into left center, splitting the alley between Hooper and Walker. Hooper made a gallant dive, but to no avail. The ball rolled to the fence, and Myers scored the first run of the game after rounding third and touching the plate.

William looked out at George. What was going through his mind? Had he thought the wind was stronger? Was he going to lose composure? How long would Carrigan stick with him?

After Eli finished his cheering and sat down, he commented, "No shutout today for your friend!"

Boston tied the score in the third.

Neither team scored in the fourth. Neither team scored in the fifth, sixth, seventh, eighth, or ninth.

Neither team scored in the tenth or eleventh—or the twelfth or thirteenth.

Brooklyn's starter, Sherry Smith, was still pitching and had allowed only six hits. George had also allowed six hits but had not allowed any since the eighth. In the top of the fourteenth, he induced Johnston to ground out to Scott. Daubert hit a routine fly to Hooper. Myers ended the inning by grounding to short, Scott easily throwing him out.

Hoblitzell led off Boston's half of the fourteenth by walking. Carrigan sent in Mike McNally to run, and Duffy Lewis laid down a perfect bunt, advancing McNally to second. Then Carrigan went to his bench, replacing Larry Gardner with seldom-used Del Gainer. Replacing the sweet-swinging left-hander with this unknown pinch hitter surprised William—and he was certain all fans were as shocked as he. There was a silence as Gainer approached the plate, followed by a growing murmur.

But within seconds the game ended, Gainer lining a clean single into left, allowing McNally to slide safely into home well ahead of Zack Wheat's desperate throw to the plate.

Boston was up in the Series, 2–0.

George had just earned a fourteen-inning complete game victory for his first World Series win.

Brooklyn held on to win the first game at Ebbets Field.

In game four, the Robins scored twice in the bottom of the first. But Boston scored three in the second, another in the fourth, one more in the fifth, and another in the seventh. Though Dutch Leonard struggled in the first, he shut out the Dodgers the remainder of the game, allowing only four hits over the last eight innings. Boston led the Series, 3–1.

Eli had given up hope. He would not attend game five in Boston—a relief for William. He had grown weary of Eli's questions and anxiety whenever Brooklyn stumbled, which was often. So it would be a silent game five, with only him and Uncle Nathan watching the teams battle and neither speaking to his neighbor.

But William was wrong.

The score was tied at one after two innings. In the bottom of the third, Brooklyn's defense faltered again, an error by Olson allowing two Boston runs to score.

"If it weren't for their fielding," Uncle said, "they'd be in this thing."

William was leaning forward, head cupped in his hands, elbows braced on his knees. *Now Uncle Nathan is turning sour! What is it about Brooklyn fans?*

He turned and looked up. "Still be in the game? Or the Series?"

"Both," Uncle answered.

William lowered his head and rolled his eyes, confident his gesture could not be seen by Uncle.

"It's over? No?" Uncle asked when Chief Meyers came to bat in the fifth. The Dartmouth student singled with two out and was stranded. Mowrey, Brooklyn's third baseman, did the same in the seventh.

Just prior to the first pitch in the eighth, William leaned back, certain Brooklyn did not have the fight to make the game interesting.

From the corner of his eye, he saw Uncle slip down in his seat, an uncharacteristic posture for him when he was garbed in his black rabbinical clothes.

"Have you made a decision?" he asked William.

"Decision?" William repeated.

"When the Series is over. With your life?"

Merkle hit a nice liner into left center that Duffy Lewis chased down and caught.

"Eli talks of his work," William replied, "how much he enjoys it. The planning, engineering, managing . . . whatever it is he does. It fulfills him. He's accomplishing something that gives him meaning, purpose."

"You felt that at Harvard, yes?" Uncle asked.

"Sometimes. Maybe. I suppose . . ." William answered, but his mind and his voice faded. He did miss Harvard—the classes, the challenging puzzles to solve. The task of reconciling theories of classroom instruction with the realities he read in the *Globe*.

The eighth inning ended with Boston leading, 4–1.

Stengel led off the ninth with a single into left.

"And then there is Merlin," William continued, "Merlin and the war. The letters he's sent. He described it as an itch, something he needs to do. Whenever he spoke of flying, it was like he was somewhere else. Kind of like Eli when he speaks of the canal. But when he arrived in Toronto, they assigned him as a mechanic. He wants to fly. Attended the classes, studied for the exam to earn his license, but they won't let him fly—they say he's too valuable on the ground, working on the planes. Still, he keeps dreaming."

"And you?"

"I have no dream." William sighed.

Zack Wheat struck out. The Sox were two outs from winning their second consecutive championship.

"Still," William said, "I may have some use."

"And that use is overseas?" Uncle asked.

William nodded. "One morning we read of France's advance. The next day of British evacuation from Gallipoli. Then German gains in the Eastern Front and their losses along the west. We'll be there eventually. I know that. But I've got nothing here. Why not join Merlin? Track him down up north and travel across the Atlantic together. I've squandered my opportunities here."

As Cutshaw walked to the plate, Uncle raised his hand and straightened his kippah. He breathed deeply and cleared his throat. "I am at a loss sometimes," he said softly, almost whispering it to William.

William turned, uncertain if he heard Uncle's words clearly.

"Life seems a wilderness, yes? In fifty years you would think I'd have figured something out. Be sure of one thing. 'He's a rabbi!' they say. 'He is wise. Surely he knows!' Yes?"

Was he speaking to himself? Was this one of Uncle's rants that somehow, cryptically, was to teach a life lesson?

Uncle moved his head side to side, shaking it violently. "No. Most definitively, no!"

Cutshaw grounded out to Janvrin at second, moving Stengel up one base.

Uncle held up his hand. "I am all right, William," he assured. "Still—it makes one wonder. Upon what premise has one built his life? Yes? You feel you have failed, William. 'Squandered,' you say . . . gone down a wrong path, perhaps . . . yes?"

Mike Mowrey, Brooklyn's third baseman, dug his right foot into the box, awaiting Shore's next pitch.

"And what if one has traveled over fifty years, William? Fifty years on a road that has led him to—where? How is one such as I to advise on the path to war or elsewhere? How is one to entrust their soul to a rabbi as confounded as I?"

William looked out toward the field, hoping to escape the discomfort he felt upon hearing Uncle speak. But the pending demoralization of the Robins was even harder to absorb.

"Master of the universe," Uncle said, "promised us a Messiah— yes? One who would come and set all right . . . correct the injustices, teach us wisdom. Righteousness will reign. There will be equity.

'The wolf also shall dwell with the lamb, and the leopard shall lie down with the kid; and the calf and the young lion and the fatling together; and a little child shall lead them. And the cow and the bear shall feed; their young ones shall lie down together: and the lion shall eat straw like the ox.'"

William consciously tried to keep his face from contorting. He would not dishonor the patriarch of this family that had given him so much.

Still, to unleash this pent-up rhetoric in the seats of Brave's Field—in the midst of the world championship! *Would someone please explain to Uncle how ludicrous it is!*

"A wolf and a lamb," Uncle muttered. "A leopard next to a kid? A calf and a lion? A cow and a bear? Did Isaiah compose such words with hope of an equitable zoo? Is this what the Messiah will accomplish? Is it not to tear apart all that we have built between us? That separates us? That divides? And has it not happened? Have I not seen it? On the plains? During their ceremony with bread and wine? Cowboys and ranchers and natives and bankers. Former slaves and politicians. Women, children, all partaking . . . all acknowledging . . . He had already come."

Mowrey hit a weak fly to short, easily caught by Everett Scott to end the game and the Series.

The crowd cheered, but certainly not as raucously as for the previous Boston wins William had witnessed. The Rooters raided the field, blasting "Tessie," while William remained seated, watching Uncle continue his deliberation.

He appeared finished but remained in the same position, leaning forward, eyes focused on the field, watching the Boston players celebrate with their fans.

As the seats emptied, Uncle turned to William. His eyes were narrowed, his brow furrowed, as if he were struggling to unravel a difficult geometric theorem.

"Well?" Uncle asked. "What do you think?"

"Of all you've been saying?"

"Yes."

William shifted his eyes away. He shook his head and before speaking focused back on Uncle. "I don't believe in any of that."

"And?"

"You know I don't. I respect and admire the teachings of the Bible—what I learned at St. Mary's, what I hear at the children's temple—just like I admire any sound moral teachings."

"Did what I speak make sense? Could you understand it?"

William stared at Uncle, measuring the possible responses he might make and determining which would more quickly end the conversation.

"Tell me, William," Uncle continued, "why do you choose to spend so much time with the Chalmerses?"

The question surprised William. He thought of how he had avoided the family since returning, yet how much he'd love to be back in their company.

"Perhaps," William replied, "their kindness. They treat me like family."

"And Merlin?"

"I suppose the same. We're friends."

"And what they believe?" Uncle prodded. "Does that not bother you? The fact that you don't believe any of that nonsense?"

William shrugged. He'd wondered this himself over the years. He could not reconcile their belief in a kind Creator with the ugliness he had experienced and lived on a daily basis. Still, he admired them and was grateful for their friendship.

"You tolerate it?"

"Yes. I suppose that's one way of putting it."

Uncle looked away, then after some moments looked back at William.

"No," he said. "I think it has more to do with your curiosity. Less about tolerance."

1917 – Reconnaissance

Their eyes looked forward, mouths were shut, arms pressed to their sides, awaiting the next command from the visiting officer. William often reminisced about these hours spent alongside his classmates, preparing for what might be. He thought of them as they congregated on the fields in Plattsburgh, dressed in khakis left over from the war with Spain fifteen years earlier. Each step they took brought them nearer to forming regimental lines as the innocence of youth transformed into expressions of anxiety and seriousness, laying the groundwork for the trenches of age that would soon leave scars.

For three hours each week they would journey north and learn how to dig trenches, tunnel, mine, set barbed wire, destroy barbed wire, and march. Once the three hours ended and they loaded back onto the southbound train, the routines awaiting them in Cambridge brought smiles back to their faces, and conversation and laughter soon filled each boxcar.

Those hours in Plattsburgh had been a nuisance. William had had scholastic responsibilities, athletic commitments. Two evenings each week he'd tutored Jenny. He had no time to play soldier.

But now, a year later, on the other side of the Atlantic and thirty feet underground, on the eve of going over the top for his first action, he yearned for those days.

Back then, they had warm beds in which to sleep—now there were no beds, or, at best, a wooden slab or sandbag to help them get rest. Back then, they returned to a cafeteria with options— sandwiches, soups, or the main dish of the day. Now they ate something that resembled a stew or porridge. Whatever it was, he would shut his eyes consuming it, wishing he could also hold his nose. Late at night, the scratching of tiny feet racing on the outside of the wooden trenches kept him awake, kept him worried that if one of the rats had grown so accustomed to human neighbors, they may seek a nighttime companion.

But it was the faces that he thought of most, the faces of his Harvard comrades. Back then, it was all going through the motions, following a set of rules, a game they were playing, a theory. Now there was nothing more real than what he and his new comrades would soon encounter. He had heard the reports of Verdun, the Somme, and the earlier battles at Ypres. What he read in the papers had filled him with rage. Now what he had seen of the effects of war assaulted his senses. Blank stares of men who had seen action. Were these veterans of the Somme and Verdun once as innocent as he? What had they seen that had soiled their eyes?

William would sit, but his pants would become saturated with mud. For weeks, torrential rains delayed major military advances from either side of no-man's-land between Roye and Reims on the Aisne River. There were artillery barrages from the big guns on both sides, creating myriads of craters dotting the landscape. Two hundred yards to the east, on the other side of the chaotic labyrinth of barbed wire, hidden in their own deep tunnels and trenches, lay the German Army.

The regret of following Merlin reared its head, but he had battled this regret many times during the past six months. He would not succumb to it on the eve of glory. He reached into his right pocket and walked toward the far corner of the trench, near the only lantern in their sector. He unfolded the picture of Brother Thomas with his three friends in front of the Ferris wheel at the Chicago World's Fair. He raised his hand and lightly touched the top of Thomas's head.

He folded the picture, returned it to his right pocket, then reached into his left pocket and unfolded a clipping from a newspaper he bought just before boarding the ship in New Brunswick. He inched closer to the lantern, squinting to read the small print:

Ruth's Run-in With Umpire

Babe pitched four balls to Morgan and accused Owens of missing two of them. "Get in there and pitch," ordered Owens.

"Open your eyes and keep them open," chirped Babe.

"Get in and pitch or I will run you out of there," was the comeback of the arbiter.

"You run me out and I will come in and bust you on the nose," Ruth threatened.

"Get out of there now," said Brick.

Then in rushed Ruth. Chester Thomas tried to prevent him from reaching Owens, who had not removed his mask, but Babe started swinging both hands. The left missed the arbiter, but the right struck him behind the left ear.

Manager Barry and several policemen had to drag Ruth off the field. All season Babe has been fussing a lot. Nothing has seemed to satisfy him.

William looked up from the article, considering the possible causes of the turmoil George was enduring. He had won two consecutive world championships. He was the premier pitcher on a staff of the best pitchers in the league. He was likely the best-hitting pitcher in the history of the game. What could be ailing his old classmate from St. Mary's?

William again leaned closer to the lantern and re-read the final line in the article: "All season Babe has been fussing a lot. Nothing has seemed to satisfy him."

And William had concluded that what ailed George was the fight in Europe in which he was not participating.

On April 2 President Wilson requested Congress to declare war on Germany, and two days later the Senate agreed. A draft was instituted, and the troops were already arriving, though most had yet to see action. Whatever circumstances were keeping George from joining the fight, it must be tearing him up inside. Perhaps his draft number had not been called, perhaps he wanted to join the ranks but the team would not allow it, or perhaps he was considering leaving the ball field nonetheless.

If George was berating himself for not fighting, William was berating himself, second-guessing his decision to find Merlin. All the letters he had sent, all the letters he received back had been addressed to the Curtiss Flying School in Toronto. Following Brooklyn's defeat to Boston, he went to the bank, withdrew one of the two remaining diamonds from the safe-deposit box, and with Uncle Nathan's assistance sold the diamond to a trusted jeweler in the diamond district for $15,000. After depositing $10,000 into his account, he packed his satchel and headed north. When he arrived at the Curtiss School, he discovered Merlin had transferred to Camp Borden, another aviation training facility in Barrie, north of Toronto. When he arrived in Barrie, he was told that Merlin had left to join the French Foreign Legion. Based on what the facility's administrators said, Merlin's departure was a disappointment to all at Barrie. He was the most dependable and efficient of mechanics. The aviators specifically asked for him to run final inspections or fine-tune whatever needed fixing.

"He left," said the president of the school, "for the same reason he left Curtiss. He wanted to fly.

"He thought," the president continued, "that Canadians would be more forgiving of his skin color. And we are. Both Curtiss and our facility taught and trained Mr. Jones—an opportunity he would not receive in your country. And he is a good flyer, a great pilot. But whenever the next group of graduates was shipped across the Atlantic, his application was not accepted.

"'His value as a mechanic is indispensable,' was the usual sentiment expressed in the denial of his requests to fly. I supposed he grew tired of waiting for us to grow blind to his color and thought he would find the French more understanding."

William boarded the first train east, then purchased a second-class ticket on the next passenger ship departing from St. John's Harbour in New Brunswick. He arrived at Le Havre on July 4, traveled south to Paris, east toward Verdun, and caught up to Merlin at Beauzée-sur Aire on the evening of July 15. He and his squadron were making final preparations to travel north to join the fighting near Ypres.

Merlin was dressed in a long beige overcoat resembling the duster Matty wore on the bench, but of much heavier cloth. Underneath the duster he wore a light blue jacket with gold buttons up to the neck, a pocket on either side of his chest, and a brown belt with a golden buckle around the waist. A thinner belt slashed across his chest and attached to the belt under Merlin's left arm, looping over his right shoulder and connecting to the belt on Merlin's back. The arms of the jacket were cuffed at the wrists, and there were another two pockets near the bottom of the jacket. The jacket, with high collars, fit snugly around his neck, and on each end of the collar was a bronze pin that appeared to be a wing. Above the right breast pocket was a larger bronze medallion, a full set of wings encircled by a wreath. He wore something similar to a sailor's hat, only made of the same light blue fabric as the jacket and laced with gold fringe around the edges. He looked important. He looked happy.

"Ducky?" he said with his voice rising, his smile growing. "Ducky, is that you?"

Merlin's dream had become a reality. Well, almost.

The administrator at Camp Borden was correct. Merlin faced no obstacles among the French and had been assigned to Escadrille #93, serving under Corporal Bullard—another Black American who had found it necessary to join the French Foreign Legion to fulfill his dream to fly. For two months Merlin had been flying reconnaissance missions, still two steps from realizing his dream of becoming a fighter pilot. In fact, he had yet to be promoted to pursuit pilot, whose main task was to drive away German reconnaissance planes and protect Allied reconnaissance efforts.

If the legion was good enough for Merlin, if it was good enough for Corporal Bullard, it would be good enough for William.

William joined the next day as Merlin and his unit flew north. One week later he joined the other legionnaires waiting in reserve to move toward the action at Ypres.

Two previous theaters had ended in catastrophe in the west Belgian village. In 1914 there were over one hundred thousand casualties among the French, British, and Belgian soldiers, and the following year another ninety thousand. Since April, the legionnaires had been placed at the rear of the reserves, waiting until their numbers had grown to a respectable, usable force. Their unit had been halved in 1915, and they continued to take heavy losses during the battles of the Somme and Verdun. Merlin, Bullard, and the other aviators serving in the Lafayette Escadrille were some of the few legionnaires that had seen action, albeit in the air, over the past several months. As William and others joined and the legion's numbers grew, the infantry units inched closer to no-man's-land.

Dawn was less than two hours away. If the rain did not return, William's unit would emerge from their holes just after sunrise. In the darkness, the colorless environs of the trenches were even more dreary. William looked down at his uniform. Like Merlin, he wore what could be described as a duster, but his was darker and was his only protection from the weather. He raised his right hand, wiggling both of the bags strapped across his shoulders, doing a quick inventory of the ammunition each contained. His soiled beige knickers and soiled white socks might display some honor and prestige when clean, but that held little concern now.

He breathed deeply and raised his head, gazing into the night—clear of clouds, clear of smoke. Each star testified that whatever happened on the fields of no-man's-land would not alter their course the following day. Such thoughts created a smile, but when he thought of the cloudless night translating into a certain morning attack, he felt the pulse of his heart accelerate, and the regrets of joining the legion returned.

"William Jennings." He heard a voice call from the other side of the trench.

Most of his fellow legionnaires called him Billy or Jennings. Whoever was beckoning him must not be part of the unit.

"William John Jennings," the voice called out louder. "Mr. William Jennings of New York."

William turned and walked toward the man calling. He raised his arm, uncertain how to respond. "That's me."

The man nodded, stopped, and turned. "Follow me," he instructed, inviting him with a sweep of his arm.

They walked to the far end of the trench, climbed up the stairs, went through the camp of the reserves and past the officers' quarters, until they reached the airfield. The man stopped at the entrance of a large tent, reached across to unlatch the cloth door, and held it open for William to enter.

Inside, at the far end of the tent, a man was turning pages, signing documents. When the man looked up, the tall candle burning on the edge of the table hardly provided enough illumination for William to make out his features. "Come forward," he requested.

The man stopped his paperwork and stood, folding his arms. William felt he was entering a period of investigation, like one of the dissertation defenses he had witnessed under Professor Murchinson's invitation. As William neared the table, the candle's flame reflected off the man's forehead, revealing his dark skin, regal nose, and examining eyes. His lips were pressed together as if he suspected William had committed some infraction of which he was not aware and was about to receive correction.

"William Jennings?" the man asked, with a heavy southern drawl.

"Yes, sir."

"You recognize the contraption on the table to your right?" he asked, pointing at a box.

William turned from attention, looked at the box and back to the man.

"Yes, sir."

"Bring it to me."

William walked to the box camera, picked it up, and walked back toward the man.

The man held out his hand.

"Remove the film," he instructed.

William turned the Watson camera to pull the plate from its side, but it was empty. He looked up, unsure how to answer.

"Is there a problem, Jennings?" the man asked.

"There is no plate, sir."

The man bent down, reached under his desk, and held out another Watson camera toward William. "Try this one."

William looked toward the table, unsure if he ought to take the time to race over and place the empty Watson back onto the table. He decided to place it carefully at his feet, then stepped forward to receive the other camera.

He received the Watson, removed the plate, and held it out, trying to preserve whatever image it contained.

"Very good," the man said, his expression easing for the first time since William entered the tent. "Mr. Jones speaks well of you."

"Sir?"

"You were scheduled for the advance this morning? At Pilckem Ridge?"

William sensed the man was not expecting an answer. So he gave a quick nod, saying nothing.

"You have been transferred to this unit. Escadrille 93."

"Yes, sir," William said, trying to contain the excitement, surprise, and relief he felt washing over each other within his chest.

"Get some rest. I wouldn't wonder if you hadn't slept, ehh?"

"No, sir. Not much."

"You will go up with Jonesy this afternoon toward the west, away from the action. See how your fingers adjust to the frigid air. Make sure your stomach survives maneuvers."

The man's lips returned to their solemn pressing action. "Don't imagine you've been airborne previously . . . ehh?"

"No, sir."

"We'll see how to proceed after your performance this afternoon."

William felt the pressure in his chest increase. He straightened his posture. "Thank you, sir."

"Corporal Bullard," the man said, smiling and extending his hand. "Welcome to our team."

***

That afternoon, Merlin ascended into the rear seat of the Breguet aircraft, instructing William to enter into the front compartment. He tried to remember how his friend had maneuvered into his perch, and as he contemplated how to get to his seat, as he considered what he could hold onto for support, he felt the sides of the plane. The metal body was smooth and cool, not at all what William had expected, hearing previously of other aircrafts' cloth-like composition.

The trepidation he felt was heightened as he witnessed Merlin's competence—competence that appeared to be so second nature. William looked on with awe and pride as his friend orchestrated his instructions with the crew on the ground, checked the instruments, maneuvered the plane onto a long dirt road, then lifted it into the air.

"You will be frightened and excited and uncertain," Merlin had warned that morning, "and we won't be able to speak. Well . . . we can try, but we likely won't hear one another."

William nodded.

"Trust me," Merlin urged. "You'll be fine."

Within minutes of leaving the ground, Merlin began his first maneuver by changing the direction of the Breguet, speeding as he turned the aircraft east, back toward the trenches of the Western Front. Then he did what William later learned was a *retournement*: Merlin accelerated the plane to a greater height, turned it downward at its apex, then quickly accelerated downward. There was the horizontal *vrille* in which the pilot tosses and turns the plane, as if to make it take flight like a glider, turning it, tipping the wings. Afterward, Merlin again steered the plane in a quick upward thrust, then just as quickly changed direction for a momentary dive, then back upward. Once at the apex, he pointed the nose of the plane back toward the ground, tipping the wings, rising momentarily, then diving.

William's stomach survived, though he was lightheaded upon returning to the ground, and he found it took several minutes before he could walk normally without leaning to the left or right to gain balance.

"You passed," Merlin declared. "Tomorrow we take photos."

At dinner, William discovered two things. First, life for the aviator was a bit more agreeable than for those in infantry or artillery units. Instead of eating porridge from tin cups and bowls, squatting or sitting on mud and dirt bumps in the trenches, William and the others in his unit sat on chairs at long tables in a structure resembling a log cabin. The food was solid, real food—poultry and potatoes and vegetables. The second discovery was that Merlin played a significant role in the corporal's decision to secure William's transfer.

On their way to the Breguet that afternoon, William heard several crew members and other pilots shout words of encouragement to Merlin.

"Congratulations," some said.

"We're rooting for you, Jonesy!" said another.

And, "You deserve it. Now go show all the others how wrong they are."

At first, William considered that the words of encouragement were a way of the unit teasing Merlin for being teamed with the new recruit—having to train a rookie reconnaissance photographer who did not know what he was getting into. Then during supper, most of the unit was silent, even avoiding contact with Merlin.

"Sorry," one pilot whispered to Merlin as they waited in line to receive their food. "I didn't know."

"You'll get another chance," said one of the men William recognized from the crew that assisted in takeoff.

Merlin did not respond to either comment, causing William to infer what had transpired prior to his arrival at the airfield.

"You had received the promotion," William whispered from the top bunk that evening, unable to fall asleep, fearful of learning the truth, waiting nervously for Merlin to reply.

He didn't.

"They promoted you to pursuit pilot?" William prodded.

Still, Merlin said nothing.

"I don't know how all this works. I don't understand all the intricacies of promotion, how you do what you do, what levels you must obtain . . . but I know you, Merlin. I know your dreams. I saw you paste those articles above your bed for two years. That look in your eyes when you spoke of planes and flying, your chance to be free, free from being constrained to the ground. Where you are told you can get an education but can't have this job. Where you can preach a sermon but could never pastor this church . . . where you can play halfback or center field, but never in this league. In the air it's different, yes?"

But Merlin did not respond.

William was certain his friend was awake. He had learned from their years at Harvard to distinguish Merlin's breathing rhythms. When asleep, there was a steady pace to his breathing. But when Merlin was awake, his breathing was barely audible.

William turned onto his side and leaned over the edge of the bunk, looking down at Merlin, "I don't want you to sacrifice—"

"Stop," Merlin said with a stern, soft whisper. He lifted his eyes and looked directly at William.

"We will not talk of this again. Ever."

William would not agree. He would not nod. He didn't want to be the reason his friend was unable to progress to the position of which he dreamed—a status he could achieve without the constraints he faced on the other side of the ocean.

"I have seen things, Ducky." Merlin said before turning his eyes away from William and staring at the door of their dormitory. "I have seen horrors that Dante could not even imagine in the lowest of his circuits.

"Men—boys younger than you and me—returning to the trench, some of the lucky few to have survived. Then at dusk, when it is safe . . . well, as safe as one could hope, they venture back to no-man's-land, searching for a lost finger, or ear, or arm, or friend. They come to the infirmary, faces lashed with metal, eyes missing, throats bleeding, an empty spot on their face where their nose once found a home . . ."

Merlin's eyes shifted from the dormitory door back to William. "You were heading there this morning. Dante's inferno, Ducky— you were entering it at dawn."

William saw Merlin's eyes moisten. He looked away from his friend for a moment and swallowed with difficulty as his throat constricted, hoping to constrain his own tears.

"What is ambition?" Merlin asked while raising his arm to wipe under his nose. "What are my dreams compared to a friend? Of what value is a dream compared to the value of a brother?"

William turned away from the side of the bed and lay on his back, his body convulsing from the sobs he was unable to control.

"We will not talk of this again. Ever," Merlin once more instructed.

"Ever."

***

The flights of Jones and Jennings produced valuable intelligence. At least that is what Corporal Bullard frequently told them in their pre-flight meetings each morning. In mid-August, their team located German artillery and infantry reserves. This information assisted the Allies in their encounter with German troops at Langemarck. For the battle at Menin Road in late September, photos of the sparse German resources helped the generals plan their attack. And so, with the aid of the photos William obtained over the fields of Polygon Wood and Broodseinde, the Allied forces were able to push the Germans further east.

William questioned how the Germans continued their attempt at supremacy. Everything he saw in the air convinced him that soon they would have to surrender. The fields to the west of the trenches were green and lush, with an endless supply of food to strengthen the Allied troops. The fields east of the trenches were dried, brown, parched. And in combination with the British blockades, resources of German military had to be dwindling to catastrophic levels.

Still, the Germans fought bravely. The war started during the summer of 1914. It was now the fall of 1917, and the gains on both sides resembled a stalemate contest in chess—an extra-inning affair well into the twentieth or twenty-first inning.

If it had not been for the heavy rains during the summer, perhaps Generals Haig and Pétain could have launched a decisive blow on the Germans. Perhaps if the Russian people had not turned against their czar and weakened the push against the Germans on the Eastern Front, the kaiser would not have been able to strengthen his defenses with reinforcements from the east. Perhaps if the rains had not continued to saturate the fields of France and Belgium, the Allied artillery could have done more damage. Perhaps if the skies were less cloudy, the reconnaissance missions could bring back more useful information.

Perhaps. Perhaps. Perhaps.

Now it was early October. Another assignment given: "Rise early. Target location of enemy machines, reserves, and guns. If weather is inclement, return immediately."

They rose at 4:00 a.m. and ate breakfast in silence. Then Merlin lifted the plane from the runway at dawn, keeping in sight their protecting pursuit plane. Within twenty minutes they were deep into German territory. Merlin turned the plane, and William reached for the camera. The clouds were thin and dispersing like the mist on a warm summer morning. Below, nothing obstructed the view. William pointed the Watson downward and began taking photos.

The rest of the day it rained. At night, the rain became a downpour. The sound of the torrent was drowned by the steady barrage of artillery shells firing and landing from both sides of no-man's-land. The developed plates from the Watson showed new positions of German troops to the east of Ypres, preparing to defend against Allied offensives.

At supper, Corporal Bullard came to their table and handed the next day's assignment to Merlin.

"More of the same tomorrow, boys," he said. "Your efforts today provided valuable intel. You pleased some very important men this afternoon."

"More of the same tomorrow" meant that he and Merlin would need to wake at 4:00 a.m. That meant going to sleep at 7:30, 9:00 at the latest.

They finished their meal and headed to their quarters.

William had already fallen asleep when he was awakened by someone holding his arm, gently rocking him back and forth.

"Wake up, William," the voice whispered.

When he opened his eyes, he saw Merlin peering at him, his arms gripping the wooden frame of the top bunk. Though his friend was smiling, William saw that he was struggling to keep his balance, straining to hold onto the edge of the wooden railing. William shuffled toward the end of his mattress and looked down, where Merlin's feet tiptoed on the frame of the lower bunk.

Merlin seemed eager and excited, like the child he'd met in Chicago ten years earlier—no traces that a war was raging several hundred yards from their sleeping quarters.

"C'mon, Ducky." Merlin shook him more vigorously. "Gotta get up!"

Merlin had clearly not yet been to sleep. His eyes were wide, resembling the game face he wore prior to running out to center field at the start of a ball game. Eager and childlike. Not at all like the game face he wore out on the airfield—his set eyes and a studious, somber expression. Seeing the old Merlin now beckoning William to awaken was enough for William to pull the sheets away and sit on the edge of his mattress.

"Happy birthday!" Merlin whispered more loudly, "Happy birthday, Ducky!"

William shut his eyes, still feeling groggy. He shook his head and said with some annoyance, "I was born in June."

Merlin released his grip on the bunk and jumped to the floor.

"It's a belated gift, Ducky. I completely forgot."

Merlin turned and raced to the dormitory door.

"Follow me," he said, holding the door open.

William pushed himself off the mattress and landed with both feet on the floor. He placed his civilian pants over the pajamas he wore and followed Merlin to the communications tent. When they entered, only two other people were inside—Corporal Bullard and a man seated behind the telegraph from which instructions were received.

The tent had been arranged with four long benches on the north side and four on the south, with an aisle leading to the telegraph operator's table.

Corporal Bullard waved Merlin to come sit with him at the front bench on the south side.

"Have a seat," the corporal invited.

Bullard was dressed in his civilian clothes and looked less imposing than normal, with his shirt hanging outside his belt.

"Have a seat, boys," he requested again. "It's about to begin."

For several minutes nothing of any significance occurred. Both Merlin and the corporal seemed to be waiting for something— likely a message with the following day's instructions. But the expressions on their faces were not expressions of work or tasks to be assigned. The corporal was biting his lip. He was dancing his fingers on his leg, making rhythm to some imaginary tune in his head. Merlin was still wearing the childlike smile he'd had when he woke William from sleep several minutes earlier.

William turned when he heard voices of other airmen approaching from behind. One of them was a fighter pilot from his unit, and the other two he recognized as some of the newly arrived

American officers. The three of them looked toward Bullard, nodded, and sat at the rear bench on the left side of the tent.

More minutes passed with silence.

William looked at the clock above the desk of the telegraph operator. It was 2010—after eight o'clock. William ought to be asleep.

"Tap, tap . . . tap, tap. Tap." A message finally arrived.

Merlin raised his head higher. The corporal straightened his already perfect posture and slid forward on the bench. He rubbed his hands together and smiled. "Here it comes," he whispered. "This is it, boys!"

The machine's clicking continued. "Tap, tap, tap . . . tap," it went on, for about thirty more seconds.

The operator cleared his throat and began speaking. "Weather, fair."

William looked over at Merlin, then the corporal. This meant lots of photos could be taken at dawn. But neither of them responded to this news. The corporal's fingers were still dancing; Merlin was still smiling like a kid.

The operator continued. "Time, zero two zero five hours."

William looked back at the members of the escadrille seated at the rear of the tent, wondering how they might respond to the news.

"Officials." The operator resumed after more tapping of the machine. "O'Loughlin. Klem. Rigler. Evans."

This woke William from his perplexity. He recognized the officials' names—they were umpires! He felt his posture straighten. He turned to Merlin, who winked as his smile grew wider.

"Hmm," the operator said as he looked up at those in the room. "Something new." His eyes shifted to the corporal. "O'Loughlin's at the plate," the operator noted, "but the others are each at a base . . . not as in years past, y'know, like one on the bases and two in the outfield. Now one at each base. Klem at first, Rigler at second, Evans at third."

The operator shrugged his shoulder, then nodded at the corporal, and the corporal nodded back.

"Hmm," the corporal muttered.

After about thirty seconds of silence, the tapping and clicking became endless. How the operator took the messages, wrote, and relayed to those in the tent the events that followed mesmerized William as much as the realization that they were receiving up-to-date accounts of what was occurring three thousand miles away on the other side of the Atlantic, just hours before the Allies would launch a new offensive against the Germans outside of Ypres.

"Cicotte's first pitch is a called strike," the operator announced. "Count is 0–1 to Giants leadoff hitter, left fielder, George Burns.

"Burns takes next pitch for ball.

"Third pitch from Cicotte is outside. Count is 2–1.

"Burns takes next pitch for strike. Count, 2–2.

"Cicotte misses again. Count is full.

"Burns sends line drive over second base bag for base hit."

William lowered his hands and rubbed them together, anticipating what McGraw would do with his leadoff man on base. He looked over at Merlin, who was no longer smiling. Cicotte was the White Sox's best pitcher, and Merlin was the White Sox's best fan.

"Next batter," the operator announced, "second baseman, Buck Herzog."

Herzog flied out to Shoeless Joe in left for the first out. Then Benny Kauff, the Giants center fielder, did the same. Burns stole second before the Giants third baseman, Heinie Zimmerman, flew out to Happy Felsch in center to end the inning. Despite the death of what had seemed to be a promising start for McGraw's team, there were two consolations for William: first, that the Giants were able to steal a bag successfully from Ray Schalk—one of the best catchers in the game—and second, the smile had reappeared on Merlin's face.

By the end of the third inning, three benches in the tent were filled as the Sox scored the first run of the Series off New York's Slim Sallee. In the fourth Happy Felsch hit a solo home run, and in the fifth the Giants scored their only run of the game. The Sox won, 2–1.

In the morning, the rain resumed its relentlessness. The planned attack at Passchendaele was postponed again. Any efforts at artillery barrage were for show. Little damage could be induced on the Germans with shells falling into mud, plopping instead of bouncing and ricocheting to incur their damaging blows. William's escadrille unit was able to find pockets of clear skies throughout the day, and he got several pictures of congregating German troops. Several of the fighters in their group dropped enough bombs to destroy a railway station the German Army used for the transport of troops and artillery.

In the evening just before nine o'clock, William and Merlin left their quarters and walked to the communications tent. Seven of the eight benches were full. As they entered, they were pushed forward by a surge of newcomers scurrying in, rushing toward the vacant spots on the benches.

William saw the corporal rise from his seat at the right front bench and, with his determined gait, walk toward the rear of the tent. He spotted William and Merlin, pointed at them and, as he walked toward the exit, beckoned them with his index finger to follow.

Within five minutes, the three of them had added another four benches inside the tent. They had missed the action of the first inning, but that was fine; neither team had scored. After Fletcher grounded to Buck Weaver at short for the first out of the second inning, the next three Giants singled, scoring two runs. William walked toward one of the empty seats at the rear of the tent and was about to sit when he noticed Merlin walk to the entrance of the tent, hold the door open, and help a soldier with crutches enter. Merlin guided the man to one of the new benches, returned to the tent's entrance, and helped another wounded soldier find a seat. As the White Sox hurler, Red Faber, pitched out the inning with no further damage, Merlin wheeled into the tent a man whose left leg was missing.

It was New York's first lead of the Series, but it didn't last long. Joe Jackson led the bottom of the second with a single; Felsch did the same. Chick Gandil singled, scoring Jackson from third; Weaver singled, scoring Felsch and tying the score. McGraw had seen enough. He yanked Schupp from the mound and replaced him with Fred Anderson. Meanwhile, Merlin had escorted another five men from the infirmary to the benches at the rear of the tent.

The third inning action on both sides was limited to a solitary single by Shoeless Joe, after which William rose from his seat and began to assist Merlin with the newly arriving wounded.

In the bottom of the fourth, the Sox hit six singles and scored five runs, forcing McGraw to replace Anderson. William, Merlin, and the corporal squeezed three more benches into the tent. As the number of men in the tent increased, the excitement, the cheering, the applause, and the laughter helped to momentarily erase the hell outside.

The Giants failed to score another run, losing the game, 7–2. They were down in the Series, 2–0. If in Europe it was the Germans scrambling to survive on the last leg of their fight, William felt that across the ocean it was the Giants struggling to compete, battling with no legs at all.

On the 8th the rain continued to delay the offensive advances the British and French were planning. On the 9th, twenty minutes after five in the morning, despite the soggy fields surrounding Ypres, the action began. The French troops captured Saint-Jean and Mangelacre, pushing the Germans deeper away from their strongholds. The fighters in William's unit were instructed to fly low and use their guns on the German units below them. Merlin flew William above the clouds in the early morning, several miles past the German lines so they could capture the positions of German artillery. The exploits of the fighters in their unit were a strong enough diversion to give them unhindered access to the skies over which they flew.

In the evening, there was no game. The rain was falling in America also.

It was difficult to sleep that night. The anger of the Germans was evident—relentless artillery throughout the late evening hours and through the morning. The explosions from the German guns harmonized with the thunder, the arriving torrents of rain, and lightning. Still, there were reports of clearer skies to the north, and Merlin and William left the airfield in the early morning, once more obtaining photos of German gun movements.

The extra day of rest must have convinced the Sox skipper, Clarence Rowland, to start Cicotte for game three. He shut New

York down for three innings, then gave up two in the bottom of the fourth. McGraw's hurler, Rube Benton, shut the Sox down for all nine innings, allowing only four singles and one double. The 2–0 shutout was boring in comparison to the Sox hit parade three days earlier, but the increased attendance in the tent continued to heighten the morale of the wounded. William missed most of the game since the seats were filled, and others standing wherever they could made it difficult to enter the tent. But even though he could not hear the operator's calls from the telegraph, within seconds, word of mouth traveled from the front to the rear of the tent, to those outside, and to those in the infirmary who were too ill to move. As William learned of the game's developments, he rushed to the infirmary to let Merlin and the wounded know of the events occurring at the Polo Grounds.

The skies were clearer the next morning even though heavy rains continued to saturate the battlefield. It seemed both sides were resigned to using the day for preparations. Artillery barrages were sounding from both sides of the trenches, but there were no infantry movements, no consolidated efforts in the air.

At night there were no seats available at any of the benches inside the tent. A congregation of officers stood on the ground between the tent and the infirmary. William resumed his place at the front entrance of the tent, ready to rush to the infirmary with a report of the game's action.

The pitching matchup was a repeat of game two: Ferdie Schupp was on the mound for McGraw, the man who had been humiliated by the Sox bats, and Red Faber pitched for the Sox. The game was scoreless until the bottom of the fourth when Benny Kauff, the Giants center fielder, hit a homer. In the fifth New York went up by two. In the seventh they scored another run. Then in the eighth,

Kauff hit his second homer of the game. Schupp was brilliant on the mound, scattering seven hits, striking out seven. If William had pen and paper, he would have begun a T-Report on the Giants hurler.

The Series was tied, 2–2.

The next morning, offensive advances began just prior to 5:30. It had rained overnight again, and the morning was clear for a second consecutive day. The British and recently arrived ANZAC units were pushing the Germans at Passchendaele. William had heard the horrific stories of Gallipoli from these Australian and New Zealand soldiers arriving in their camp. Their experience and bravery boosted the morale of all the men. Along with the French and Belgian troops further north who were also gaining ground on the German forces, it felt like real progress was finally being made.

The thunder from the storm once more mingled with the thunder from both sides' artillery barrages. The Germans were retreating east, making no major counterattacks, only occasional raids during the evening. The weather continued to deteriorate, again allowing only pockets of opportunity to catch glimpses of action on the ground.

William would not speak to Merlin of what he felt was the futility of their missions. Any futility he felt was nothing, he knew, compared to the futility of going over the top as just one pawn in the hands of the Allied generals. So he kept his mouth shut. But he knew Merlin was frustrated as well. His eyes were low, his head was not raised, and his shoulders were not directly under his ears but several inches ahead, as though he were a turtle plodding down a road. He considered calling Merlin Tortoise, as Merlin had once monikered him Ducky, but recognized that keeping his mouth shut was the best possible decision he could make, given the circumstances.

Still, as nine o'clock approached, the subtle smile emerged on Merlin's face. William followed him to the infirmary. They were not prepared for the chaos—medics and nurses running in and out, frantic looks of being overwhelmed and helpless. At once, they knew they could not enter. The lives of men who had fallen in battle were now being fought for by the medics. Of what value could the reports from the game at South Side Park in Chicago be in comparison?

"Ahh, Mr. Jones!" A voice from outside the tent called out.

"Mr. Jennings." Another voice joined.

"Come. You must help us," said a third man.

Amidst the drawls of newly arriving wounded from the battlefields of Passchendaele, the Australians, New Zealanders, and East Indians would certainly have no interest in the contest between McGraw's Giants and the White Sox. But these men, who were apparently making a strong recovery, who had been sweating profusely two days earlier on the eve of their eternity, were now smiling, stepping forward, begging for Merlin and William to resume their services during game five of the World Series.

"You'll tell us—yes?" one of the men asked, struggling to keep his balance against the outside of the infirmary tent.

Merlin nodded. "Certainly."

William turned and raced to the communication tent.

The Sox starter, Reb Russell, pitched four straight balls to start the game.

William turned and reported to Merlin and the three men.

Buck Herzog struck a single, and Benny Kauff hit a double, scoring Burns. By the end of the opening frame, the Giants, who had not allowed the Sox to score a run for the last twenty-two innings, had taken an early lead. Perhaps, William hoped, McGraw would win another championship for the city. He raced back to his friends, and while trying to hide his joy for Merlin's sake, reported, "The Giants have taken a 2–0 lead."

Slim Sallee allowed a run in the third, but the Giants scored another two in the fourth, giving them a 4–1 lead. In the sixth the Sox scored another run. William was overjoyed, as excited as he was when he ran bats from the plate back to the dugout for McGraw's boys. "Only nine more outs," William heard himself mutter, "and we'll be one win away from the championship!"

But as he stood at the communication tent, a horror began to unmask itself in the bottom of the seventh: Jackson singled, Felsch singled, Gandil singled. It was all beginning to sound so familiar, like the nightmare in game two. After two costly errors and four more hits, by the end of the eighth the score had transformed from a 5–2 Giants lead to the Sox leading, 8–5. After the Giants were retired in order in the ninth, the Sox held a 3–2 Series lead.

On the morning of the 15th, reports of heavy German bombing at Dunkirk sombered the mood of William's unit. By the afternoon, reports arrived that continued artillery attacks and infantry advances had pushed the Germans even further east. In the air Merlin spotted a captive balloon used by the Germans for observation, approached it cautiously, then signaled William to lower his camera to the floor of the plane and pick up the gun. Two rounds was all it took. Within minutes, the large ball of fabric was floating to the earth like a mammoth tablecloth let loose from Jack's giant in the clouds.

"Ducky!" Merlin shouted into the air, loud enough for William to recognize the laughter and joy with which it was spoken. "My man, Ducky! You did it!"

When they landed, Merlin jumped from his compartment, hugged William, patted him repeatedly on the back, rubbed the top of his head, hugged him again, and said, "Now, if the Sox can hold off McGraw's men tonight, it will be a perfect day!"

Back at the Polo Grounds, Benton was on the mound for New York, Faber for Chicago. In the fourth the Sox scored three. In the fifth New York chalked up two. In the ninth Chicago added one. And when the last out of the ninth was recorded, the Giants had lost their fourth World Series.

William was sad.

Merlin was happy.

The men outside the infirmary were silent, wondering, perhaps, as William wondered, whether this had been their final whiff of the game.

1918 - Heroes

—∞—

Ring Lardner had been to Europe, somewhere on the Western Front, searching for stories, and had returned home around the same time the '17 Series had ended. Despite Merlin's efforts at pleading with the corporal, he was unable to meet the great sportswriter.

He had it all figured. "I'll track him down," he explained to William, "have him sign a newspaper, any paper, even if it's in French. Pops will get a kick—he'd love it!"

There was a list of reasons why Merlin and his father were fans of Lardner. "Well, for starters," Merlin once told William, "he's funny, though he doesn't flaunt his humor. It's subtle. Then there's his coverage of the three-game exhibition between the Cubs and Foster's Giants back in '09. But the biggest reason is Lardner's esteem for Pop's favorite player, John Henry 'Pop' Lloyd of Chicago's American Giants. Back in '14, in the midst of a mediocre Cubs season when Hank O'Day was manager, Lardner wrote a poem that Pop quoted so often, I've memorized it."

Merlin often spoke the words in a whisper as he went about a seemingly mundane task, during fielding practice or working on a plane on the airstrip:

If I were Hank, I b'lieve that I
Would go out south some night,
And there corral a certain guy
Named Lloyd and paint him white.

It was several months later, after Lardner had returned to the States, when the corporal approached Merlin and William with a special mission. "I promise," the corporal declared, "it will make up for the lost opportunities of meeting Mr. Lardner."

That sounded promising. Promising enough for William and Merlin to look at one another with looks of skeptical hope.

"You will transport cartons of masks to Hanlon Field and teach gas drills to some of the arriving Americans."

Merlin pursed his lips and smiled at William. It helped ease William's skepticism, but he was sure Merlin shared his doubt that anything of value might be awaiting them in the field southeast of Paris, anything that could compensate for the missed opportunity of meeting Lardner.

But the corporal was true to his word. Once the masks were unloaded and the requisitions signed by the receiving American officers, William and Merlin were led inside the officer quarters, where they would receive instructions on the gas training drill in which they would participate.

The men inside were standing around the coffee dispenser, drinking and talking and laughing. They were each wearing the doughboy costume, as the members of William's escadrille unit had named the American uniform: a plain brown sailor-like cap, brown belt, high-necked blue jacket, and boots up to their knees. When they entered, William and Merlin stopped, looked at one another, and froze, uncertain how to approach the men who had turned to look at them.

"Mr. Jennings," the tallest man said as a smile grew on his handsome features. "Mr. William Jennings—my favorite of all the kids that served under McGraw. How are you? How long have you been here? Where are you stationed?"

William tilted his head toward Merlin. "It's Matty," he whispered.

Merlin nodded and prodded William forward. "And Cobb," Merlin muttered as he followed in William's wake.

"Boys." Matty held out his hand, shaking William's hand first, then Merlin's.

"This is—" William started before Matty interrupted.

"Merlin Jones. Quick moving, elusive back of the Crimson eleven."

"This is Mr. Cobb." Matty moved aside, allowing the boys to meet Detroit's outfielder.

William was uncertain whether he could presume to approach Cobb without Cobb's approval, but Cobb extended his hand, even squeezed William's shoulder. "Nice to meet you, boys," he said, before nodding at Merlin.

Merlin extended his right hand toward Cobb, but Cobb turned his back to refill his empty mug.

It was an awkward moment. Merlin lowered his eyes, but Matty disrupted Cobb's gesture by ushering William and Merlin toward another man whom William did not recognize.

"This is Major Branch Rickey." Matty held out his hand, inviting Rickey to step forward. The diminutive, somewhat plump man looked serious, intense, but kindly. His sturdy gaze examined William and Merlin. He pushed his spectacles closer to his eyes and smiled, extending his hand and enveloping it around Merlin's hand that had been ignored by Cobb, holding it in a tight grip for several moments.

"An honor to meet you Mr. Jones," Rickey said. "A Harvard man. Always an honor to meet a man of Crimson, yes? Red is the color of bravery. Of sacrifice."

Matty chuckled.

William looked at Merlin to gauge whether Cobb's gesture had left any scars, but Merlin was looking across at Major Rickey, engaging him in conversation. "And you, Major?" Merlin asked. "Certainly not Harvard. Otherwise, you'd have no need to look upon me with such honor."

Rickey bowed his head. "Ohio Wesleyan," he answered, "and nowhere near the talent you possess, Mr. Jones. Couldn't hit my weight and couldn't throw a runner out from behind the plate. Gave up the game on the field, got my degree, returned to the game wearing an office suit rather than the field uniform."

While Matty, Cobb, and the other officers in the Chemical Warfare unit readied their gear for the upcoming drill, Major Rickey explained to William and Merlin their responsibility. "The boys will have finished their morning drills and been led into the airtight chamber. We've been through the routine—placing the device over their head, securing the tube, clipping it into the mask, and ensuring that it is airtight. They've been through the motions countless times."

The major paused and glanced at Merlin, then William. It seemed he was waiting for some sign of their understanding before he continued. They nodded, and Rickey proceeded. "This group will experience the release of gas for the first time. They are a wild bunch. Cocky and arrogant. Many have exhausted their reprieves, and this is their last stop or they get shipped back home. It's a bit unpredictable how they may react once they realize the deadly aroma is in the air."

Again, William and Merlin nodded. They also had been through similar training.

"You are there to assist the men having difficulty. But mostly to serve as guides—an example of calm."

Ten minutes later, the trainees filed into the air chamber. By their expressions, it seemed to William they were not taking the drill seriously. Some of them entered into their formation in a sauntering walk, shoulders drooping. Some were laughing and tussling with their mates. Once the doors of the chambers closed, the lines straightened and there was silence. A man near the front of the chamber raised his hand and made a circling motion, similar to an umpire's call of a home run. It was the signal Rickey instructed Merlin and William to look for—the signal for the release of gas.

A mad scramble ensued amongst the lines of soldiers. As William raised his hands to affix the mask and ensure it was properly secured, he observed mixed reactions among the ranks. Most, like him, reacted calmly. Others looked from side to side and started fidgeting, reaching to secure their helmets, but, unable to do so, their panic worsened. Some began shuffling their feet, moving around in a strange dance, like they were running in place. Still others fell to their knees and began their struggle to figure out the device.

Matty turned toward Major Rickey.

William wondered whether the unfolding chaos was normal. Major Rickey was helping one of the panicked men secure his mask. In the far corner of the chamber, Matty was helping another soldier. Within seconds all the lines broke formation, and soldiers were racing for the one exit in the chamber.

William and Merlin were left alone, standing at the far end of the chamber. They looked at one another, and though they couldn't see each other's face but only the awkward mask, they shrugged, uncertain what had just happened.

While most of the men in the chamber were fighting to make an exit, several were not. Eight of the trainees were on the floor coughing, choking on the gas. Matty had circled his arm around the man he was assisting and found him a place in the exit line. William noticed that Matty was fidgeting with his mask and that its tube was not securely fastened into its proper location. He was coughing, bending over, hacking, and struggling to breathe as he dragged the trainee toward the exit.

***

A chorus had emerged—a list of tragedies, similar to the lyrics of "The Twelve Days of Christmas," only instead of the twelve drummers, eleven pipers, and on down to the partridge, it was a litany of events that had gone askew in the career and personal life of the great Giants pitcher. The increased potency was the stuff of the Bible, like the trials of Job or the struggles of Joseph. William replayed the image of Matty in the air chamber, bent over and coughing, while still attempting to help the young soldier by his side. He played the images over and over in his memory as Merlin flew the plane north, back toward their unit near the Ypres salient.

If he had his collection of T-Reports, he would extract the ten pages he kept on Matty and add the incident he and Merlin just witnessed. Matty's life had become a Shakespearean comedy, with each new act adding to the absurdity of the drama.

The year following his three shutout performances in the '05 Series, he battled diphtheria. In '08 there was the blunder by Merkle, leading to the loss of the one-game playoff; during the off-season, his youngest brother, Nicholas, shot himself. In 1911 there was the bad pitch to Baker; in 1912 the dropped pop-up by Snodgrass and Speaker's foul pop that dropped between Matty, Myers, and Merkle. In '13 the loss in game five transpired; in Cincinnati he took over one of the worst teams in the National League, and within two seasons they became one of the best. Still, he was challenged by the most corrupt player in the game—Hal Chase, the star, sharp-hitting first baseman—who not only threw games when it was convenient, but encouraged and pressured teammates to do the same. And as the team improved, William read sportswriters' impressions of the situation—that Matty was waiting for his opportunity, gathering evidence and turning it over to the authorities, finally ridding the team of Chase's influence. As the Reds continued to improve, Matty volunteered to go overseas. Around the same time, his other brother, Henry, died from tuberculosis.

Still, Matty smiled. Still, Mr. Mathewson treated teammates and strangers with kindness. Still, Christy was the best hurler that William believed would ever pitch in either league.

***

The Germans had become increasingly unpredictable. On the ground they had become fierce, defending the places they still held. But when they were not defending, they were in retreat as the Allies pushed eastward against the Hindenburg Line. In the air there was a vindictiveness, a desperation to erase as many Allies as possible from the skies, whatever the cost.

On Thursday, September 5, the Allies enjoyed major victories along 130 miles of German defenses in Coucy, Canal du Nord, Ailette, and just north of Soissons. This continued on through September, just as the Series had ended on the other side of the Atlantic.

As William was taking photographs of the deteriorating resources of the German Army, he imagined the thoughts dancing through the mind of George, three thousand miles to the west.

President Wilson had decreed that "baseball must go on!" And so it did, though the season was shortened and the Series began earlier, on the same day the Allies had their string of victories along the Hindenburg Line. As a celebration of the Allied victories on the 5th of September, William, Merlin, the corporal, and the other Americans in their camp congregated as they had eleven months earlier in the communications tent to listen to the narration of Boston's ace pitcher, George "Babe" Ruth, pitch a six-hit shutout against the Chicago Cubs at Comiskey Park. William was fairly certain that the Cubs had wanted to maximize ticket sales, which would explain the games being played at the home of their crosstown rivals.

On the 6th of September, after Germany announced martial law in Berlin and after another sixty-mile line of German defenses was pushed further east, Chicago's Lefty Tyler beat Bullet Joe Bush, 3–1, evening the Series at one.

On Saturday General Pershing led American troops to gain a stronghold on the Aisne. That evening in the communications tent, the telegraph operator narrated as Boston's Carl Mays beat the Cubs, 2–1, giving the Sox a 2–1 Series lead.

As British and French troops were closing in on Saint-Quentin, George was preparing for the most memorable game of his career. In the top of the third, he picked off from second base the Cubs leadoff man, Max Flack. In the bottom of the fourth, he hit a two-run triple, giving the Sox a 2–0 lead. In the top of the fifth, he stopped a hard grounder up the middle and threw to his shortstop, Everett Scott, to turn an inning-ending double play. In the top of the seventh, after walking two batters, he induced another inning-ending double play. In the bottom of the seventh, he laid down a sacrifice bunt. In the top of the eighth, Chicago finally got their first runs of the Series off George, tying the game at two, but rather than remove George, Boston's manager, Ed Barrow, moved him to left field and replaced him on the mound with Bullet Joe Bush. Bush retired the Cubs in the top of the eighth, Boston scored one in the bottom of the frame, and Bush retired the Cubs again in the ninth, giving the Sox a 3–1 Series lead.

The next morning Merlin flew deep into German territory, and William captured photographs of German artillery being amassed to defend Saint-Quentin. That evening Chicago narrowed the Series, beating Boston, 3–0, behind Hippo Vaughn's pitching.

There was a lull along the trenches on September 11. Perhaps William imagined it was in anticipation for Boston's pending victory. And indeed, Carl Mays pitched brilliantly once more, beating the Cubs, 2–1, and giving the Red Sox their fifth world championship.

***

Two months later, on November 11, as the Germans continued to retreat toward their homeland, Merlin and William were given the assignment to report the enemy's most westward and eastward positions.

There had been animated whispers that Germany was on the brink of surrender. Rumors circulated that an armistice could be signed later in the day and an unwritten agreement existed between the two sides to suspend fighting.

Still, their team had been tasked to do what they had done over the past two years. They were escorted by two pursuit pilots in Nieuport 17s and two fighters in aircraft developed by the French company, Société pour l'Aviation et ses Dérives, nicknamed SPADs by those in the unit. The SPADs led the unit southeast over the Belgian town of Charleroi, where the Germans had enjoyed an early victory over the Allies during the first year of the war. Nothing of any significance was noted by William. The fields were dry, some were scorched, but there was no movement of troops and, most notably, few signs of any German artillery on the ground.

As they passed over the east Belgian town of Namur, the lead pilots turned north and tipped their wings, signaling the rest of the unit to turn homeward. The pursuit pilots elevated their Nieuports and continued their eastward flight, allowing Merlin to fall between the SPADs and Nieuports.

William heard the humming of the distinctive German motor about two minutes after they had turned westward. Several seconds later the humming became a melody, and from the northeast, through the clouds over northern Belgium, five enemy aircraft dispersed into a circular formation.

Before the SPADs had time to react, the German fighters had fired several rounds, sending both SPADs into a spiraling descent, their impact creating clouds of fire and smoke to the right of Merlin and William. The Nieuports raced from behind and caught two of the German attackers head-on, also sending them to the ground.

William looked to his left and saw what appeared to be their German counterpart biding its time. William braced himself when he felt the motor accelerate and Merlin began his retournement maneuver. As Merlin lifted the Breguet to whatever apex he deemed appropriate, William reached for the automatic rifle and tried to gain his bearings, calculating north, south, east, west.

When Merlin coasted the motor, William could see that below them one of the Nieuports was hit. In its free fall, the Nieuport aligned its descent into one of the three remaining German aircraft. Both planes burst into flames as the Nieuport impacted the enemy.

Merlin had instructed William for an occasion such as this. "Aim for the prop," he had tutored. "Aim for the propeller. Send them on the uncontrollable journey."

William settled the gun, waiting for a clear shot while Merlin did the unexpected. Rather than complete his retournement, midway down he entered into his change of direction maneuver, thus confusing William, but certainly confusing the enemy. And within ten seconds, William recognized the benefit of Merlin's choice. Directly before them was the last German attacker. William fired the gun, killing the German propeller and sending the aircraft onto its "uncontrollable journey."

But as William successfully downed the last German fighter, the Breguet's counterpart had downed the escadrille's last Nieuport. William turned the gun to his right and fired at the German reconnaissance plane as they fired back at the Breguet.

A dogfight ensued between the two recons.

Again, Merlin raised the plane into a retournement, this time completing the course and allowing William an open shot from behind the last German aircraft.

William aimed at the propeller.

Moments later the German plane began to cough and smoke. The German photographer turned and fired several shots directly into William's face, but Merlin dipped the plane, and as William shut his eyes, awaiting the pain the German artillery would create, he felt nothing—no impact. Merlin's maneuver allowed them to slip under the German aircraft and continue their journey west.

***

They had been hit.

Smoke and sputtering from the engine forced William to turn away, coughing, choking, and gagging. He turned to look at Merlin. His friend's expression was stoic. He looked past William as if he weren't seated in front of him. He looked to the left, to the right, back to the left, down at the ground, then shook his head violently as if he were trying to keep himself from falling asleep.

Within two minutes, Merlin guided the plane to land in a field on the banks of the Sambre River, avoiding the barns and homes in the neighboring fields.

When the wheels contacted earth, the plane bounced once, hit ground again, and rolled several hundred yards before it came to rest about a home run's distance from the Sambre. William jumped from the front unit onto the lower wing and realized the engine was not running. Either it had been destroyed by the Germans or Merlin had shut it off. He looked back at Merlin, expecting him to be fiddling with the instruments in the rear unit, but he was not moving. His head was lowered, tilted toward the right, and his eyes were closed.

"Merlin!" William shouted as he hopped back to the outside of Merlin's compartment, grabbed his shoulder, and shook him. "Merlin!"

He raised his head, seemingly with great effort, and slowly opened his eyes. "Hey, Ducky," he said, as the corner of his mouth struggled to rise to a smile. "We land safely?"

"You landed safely, buddy! You saved our lives!"

Merlin raised his head and lowered it, a weak attempt at a nod. "That's good," he whispered, then closed his eyes and lowered his head onto his right shoulder.

William shook him once more. "Merlin! Merl!" he shouted. "Wake up! We've got to get out of here before the Germans find the plane."

But he didn't move.

"Are you injured? Have you been hit?"

Still, Merlin didn't budge.

William lifted himself into Merlin's compartment and raised his friend from the seat, struggling to push him above the rim of the unit and onto the wing. Once he had removed Merlin, he saw the blood—the pool of blood on the seat, on the floor, sprayed against the sides of the unit. He looked down at Merlin, curled up on the wing like an infant asleep in a crib. Blood was everywhere, saturating his pants and uniform. There were two tattered holes through his jacket in the chest area. His legs were punctured with ragged holes.

He jumped from the compartment and onto the wing next to Merlin, then held him under his arms, leaning as far as he could from the edge of the wing in order to minimize the distance from which he would have to release his friend to the ground.

William looked eastward. He saw miles of farmland, with two distant structures on the horizon—a barn, maybe, or a home. To the south, farms. To the west, farms. To the north was the river.

It was too far for Merlin to walk. William hoisted Merlin onto his shoulders and trudged northward. Five minutes later he lowered Merlin several feet from the bank of the river, removed Merlin's coat, jacket, and undershirt to get a better look at his friend's injuries. He had to do something. Anything. He wrapped the undershirt around his right hand and raced to the riverbank, dipped it into the Sambre, then returned to Merlin.

"Ducky," Merlin beckoned. "Ducky . . . come here . . ."

William raised the wet shirt to Merlin's forehead, but his friend shrugged it away. "Never mind that," he instructed. "Reach into my pocket . . . my left pocket."

William dropped the shirt and reached into Merlin's left pants pocket.

"There's a folded paper there," Merlin said through coughing and wheezing. "Did you find it?"

William unfolded the paper.

"You recognize it, Ducky?" Merlin asked, his eyes wide and his smile offering William some hope that all might be well.

"It's from the symphony. That night in Chicago," Merlin murmured. "The day we met. The Sox beat the Cubs . . . remember? The best day of my life . . ."

Merlin's eyes closed. He reached for William's hand that held the paper. He wrapped his hand around William's, cupping it inside his grip.

"I wanted us to go together. To all those places. After this was over. But now . . . now . . . you go . . . for us both. Yes?"

Merlin shut his eyes. His head lowered again, and as it rested on his right shoulder, his hands still resting on William's, he smiled.

Merlin's grip vanished, his hands limp.

William would not let go.

He pulled his friend's arms.

He pulled, but there was no response. He shook Merlin, and his body did not react.

He pulled again. He shook once more.

Pull and shake. Pull and shake.

William stood, placed his hand over his mouth, and looked up into the clearing sky.

The trees on the bank of the river rustled in the breeze, their leaves dancing. Birds were making music. The melody of the river's current joined in. All of them were oblivious. None of them cared.

William grew conscious of the sounds. Grew angry and bitter that none of them stopped to consider. And as the rhythm continued, as the cycle of leaves rustling, birds rollicking, and water dancing rolled on, William grew conscious of his own breathing, berating himself for joining the chorus of nature around him.

The cycle was disrupted by the metallic click of a Luger pistol.

"Aufstehen!" a voice shouted. "Up!"

William would not look back. He felt the cold of the pistol's metal chilling the back of his neck.

"Umdrehen!" the voice commanded. "Turn around!"

When William turned, he saw what he assumed must be a German infantry officer—certainly not one of the pilots they battled minutes earlier. His uniform was tattered, perhaps by military skirmishes, but probably more by the skirmishes with time, as if he was a child whose mother had not washed her child's clothes in several months.

The German was pointing the Luger at William's chest.

"Friederich!" the German shouted as he waved his hand, instructing another German several feet away to step forward.

"Pistole," he ordered Friederich. "Seitenwaffe."

Friederich stepped up to William, unbuckled the holster on William's side, and removed his sidearm.

"Kugeln!" the officer instructed Friederich.

Friederich emptied William's gun of its bullets, threw them into the river, and handed William's gun to the officer.

William eyed Friederich, admiring the distance he had made the bullets fly. He shifted his eyes back to the officer, awaiting his fate.

"Und das beutel." The officer looked at Friederich and lightly punched himself once on the left side of the chest and once on the right in the approximate locations where William held his reserve ammunition pouches.

William looked past the officer to the Breguet. He saw another German soldier climbing on the wings, searching from the front unit to the rear unit.

Friederich again stepped close to William, unbuckled the left ammunition pouch, threw those bullets into the river, then removed the bullets from the right pouch and threw them even further into the midst of the Sambre.

William felt himself grinning and tried to control the grin from growing. His best friend had just died. He was being captured by the enemy, and at best, he would be taken prisoner; at worst, he would be executed. And still, here he was, finding amusement in the fact that Friederich had displayed a strong throwing arm—a German, nonetheless, who likely had never stepped onto a ball field, who likely did not even know what the game of baseball was. But wasn't Honus Wagner of German descent? And Heinie Groh? Heinie Zimmerman? Heinie Wagner? And how many others? Perhaps Germans bred something into their children that contributed to their arm strength.

"Durchsuche ihn!" the officer instructed Friederich.

Friederich for the third time stepped close to William. He reached into his pants pockets, then checked all the pockets in his jacket and all the various bags around his waist and the belts across his chest.

"Nichts," Friederich informed his officer, spreading his arms, moving his head side to side.

The officer lowered his weapon and placed it in his holster.

He stepped close to William and held out William's gun in his hand, inviting him to take it. "Fertig," the officer said, looking at William less threateningly. "Der krieg ist fertig . . . fertig."

William shook his head. He looked to Friederich, hoping he might assist.

"Over," the officer said.

"The war is over," Friederich added.

The officer was still holding the gun in front of William.

William nodded, reached for his gun, and placed it into his holster.

The officer looked down at Merlin and knelt at his side. He placed his fingers at Merlin's neck, then on his wrists, then forced open his eyes. He reached for the crumpled top of Merlin's uniform and shook it, raised Merlin's torso, and placed it back onto Merlin, buttoning it to the top. He placed his right hand near the top of Merlin's uniform and ran his hand down, brushing away dirt, straightening wrinkles.

"Friederich!" the officer shouted. "Winken Karl . . . sag ihm, er soll die schaufel mitbringen."

Friederich ran toward the Breguet and shouted for Karl.

Several minutes later Friederich and Karl returned, each carrying a shovel.

As they began to dig, the officer bent over Merlin and straightened his legs. He looked over at William and motioned with a nod of his head for William to move to the other end of Merlin's body.

Friederich and Karl were efficient. Within minutes, a six-by-three-by-five grave had been dug. The officer and William laid Merlin inside.

"Warten!" Karl shouted, pointing at the pins on Merlin's chest.

The officer nodded and motioned for Karl to enter the grave.

Karl crawled inside the hole he had just dug, unpinned the metallic wings on Merlin's uniform, crawled back out of the grave, and walked to William, holding out his hand and nodding, encouraging William to take the pins.

The captain waited for William to accept the wings from Karl, then turned to Friederich and nodded.

Friederich bowed his head, said a short prayer, reached inside his shirt pocket, took out a little black book, and began reading.

"Jehova ist mein Hirte . . . mir wird nichtsch werde mangeln . . ."

As Friederich continued reading, William recognized the cadence of the Twenty-Third Psalm.

"Und ich werde wohnen im Hause Jehovas auf immerdar."

When Friederich finished, William unfolded the symphony program that Merlin had handed him minutes earlier and muttered softly, "Brahms—Germany, Sjögren and Aulin—Sweden, Rubenstein—Russia, Liszt—Hungary, Sauret—France, Paganini—Italy, Borowski—Poland."

He'd memorized them long ago. He did not need the program to serve as an itinerary.

He knelt at the edge of Merlin's grave and laid the sheet of paper on the center of his chest.

1919 – Windows and Doors

he German officer shouted, "Uns zum zug folgen?"

It sounded as though it were a question, but it also was asked with a hint of authoritarian frustration, and William looked over at Friederich and Karl, wondering how they would react to their superior.

"We go . . . north," Friederich interpreted, "to train. You follow. Yes?"

William nodded, and once the three Germans picked up their gear and turned north, William followed.

His plan was to travel to Berlin. If the war was over, something he would need to confirm, then he ought to be free to travel. He ought to be free from his obligations to the legion, to the corporal, and to the escadrille. And as far as they knew, he was dead, just as Merlin and the rest from their unit were. He was not needed; he would not be missed. From Berlin he would travel to Stockholm, from Stockholm to Leningrad, then to Warsaw, Budapest, Rome, and back to Paris, fulfilling Merlin's wish.

But when they reached the station at Namur, William changed his plans.

The war was over—this was a certainty. The polka bands and the dancing, merchants distributing wine and bread and pastries without regard for reimbursement, the children shouting and singing as if it were Christmas morning, young men and women hugging and kissing, mothers weeping, old men shuffling to the beat of the tuba and other horns, German soldiers participating alongside the Belgians—all was evidence that the four years of destruction had come to an end.

Merlin would have dived into the center of the celebratory atmosphere. William would not. He looked to his left and saw a train begin to pull out from the station. The sign on the back of the rear car read Antwerpen.

Without hesitation, William sprinted, grabbed hold of the iron railing that led up the stairs of the rear car, and jumped, pulling himself onto the bottom step. He looked back at Friederich, Karl, and the officer.

He waved, cupped his hands over his mouth and shouted, "Danke!"

During the one-hour trip to Brussels, William set his itinerary. From Brussels, he would remain on the train to Antwerp. Once the train arrived, he would walk from the station to the port. Ever since he was eight years old, when he had learned from Mr. Chalmers's letter that in Antwerp his mother had boarded a ship for America, he had hoped to come to the city and find shards from his past. The maps he had studied indicated that the distance between the train depot and the port was less than three miles. Maybe he could research records in the library and look through old newspapers. It was a long shot, but he was this close, and he had never thought it would be possible to venture here, not with the city being so deep into German territory.

Once the train reached Brussels, as passengers disembarked and new passengers entered, William stared, mesmerized at the flow of human traffic. Passengers entering and passengers exiting. They were citizens, not infantry, carrying luggage, not artillery. Within hours of the armistice, normalcy was returning.

He turned from the window and felt an overwhelming surge of exhaustion, as if his body had finally acknowledged that the need for action had ended. If it were possible, he would have talked to Merlin, discussed what they would do when they got home, talked of plans to return to college. He fell asleep, not waking until an hour later.

When he woke, the train was empty. Several feet away stood the conductor, just looking at him. He seemed to have been waiting for William to wake—perhaps waiting as a gesture of gratitude for emancipating the country. William nodded. "Merci," he said, standing and walking out onto the platform.

The celebration William witnessed in Namur was a mere prologue compared to what he heard outside in the streets of Antwerp. Even before he exited the station, he could see the crowds filling the streets. He would have to push through the mob if he were to reach the other end of the city to the port where his mother had boarded a ship twenty-one years earlier.

He made it across the first avenue with relative ease. Most of the people stepped aside when they saw him—bowing their heads and smiling. Others walked up to him, shaking his hand or wrapping their arms around him, some kissing him on the cheek. A middle-aged woman even kissed him on the lips. The tattered escadrille uniform he wore still had enough pomp and color and prestige to garner the respect and gratitude that paved his way through to the other side.

He turned to gain his bearings, making sure he began his trek in the right direction. As he turned, a beautiful large storefront window reflected the chaos behind him. He turned back toward the mayhem and smiled. Joy had been made indiscriminate—it belonged to man and woman, young and old, Belgian and German.

He looked to his left. Another large clear window gave view of the wares being sold.

Further to his left he saw that all the shops, as far as the avenue extended, showcased their merchandise through large pieces of glass.

He looked to his right—one beautiful, shiny window after another.

These were not ordinary windows that he would see in Manhattan displaying clothes or bicycles, or toys, or wigs, or kitchenware. Inside these displays—all of them—were diamonds. Diamonds on rings, necklaces, bracelets, and earrings, and some were just big chunks of stone encased in large felt boxes.

William walked to his left two blocks and came to a window that was not as shiny, not as clear, and had fewer jewels than the others he had passed.

He stopped.

Froze.

His heart raced, and it felt like it may penetrate through his chest during its next pump of blood.

He stepped closer to the window.

Behind the glass, a quilt fit snugly on a bed. To the left of the bed, a second quilt was displayed, its ends tied to two tall wooden poles that extended the quilt to its maximum length.

William looked from the bed's quilt to the one between the poles.

The beat of his heart heightened.

He took another step and felt his nose graze the glass.

There was a scene woven into both quilts—a scene he had previously seen.

Whenever he had held the quilt given to him by Eli, he wondered what the scene portrayed. Now he was captivated. How could these two quilts behind the glass have the same scene as his quilt, folded tightly and resting in his safe-deposit box back home in the bank on Wall Street? He placed his hand over his eyes, cutting the glare from the station lights on the other side of the street, confirming that what he now saw on the bed and between the poles displayed the same simple farmhouse as his quilt back home—the same two chimneys, the same large field surrounded by a tall brick wall.

Now William pressed his face against the glass, his eyes dancing. He stepped back to get a panoramic view and saw his reflection, his mouth wide. He became keenly aware, keenly ashamed, that he was supposed to be a man, a soldier, a legionnaire, a hero. Yet here he stood, like a child, wanting to escape into the world portrayed in the quilts, to magically wrap himself inside the warmth of one of them and live in a world in which it did not matter whether you had parents, a world prior to his realization that life was dangerous outside the walls of St. Mary's, cruel in the streets of Manhattan, and absurd in the fields of Belgium. He wanted to return to his bed at St. Mary's, listen to Sir Thomas read a Napoleon passage from

War and Peace, and get lost in an adventure written on the pages of a book.

As his imagination raced, his gaze fixed on the quilts. It was as if he were looking into a murky mirror, seeing a reflection of himself, not the self that stood outside the shop on the streets of Antwerp, but as a child staring back from the other side of who he had become, his legs dangling from the edge of the bed.

Movement on the other side of the glass startled him.

He stepped further back, frightened that the boy he imagined had come to life.

He heard tapping on the glass and realized a little girl was waving at him, beckoning him to enter.

She hopped from the display to the entryway and cracked open the door.

"Monsieur. S'il vous plaît. Entrez."

Two years in Western Belgium had introduced William to basic words and French phrases. Though the girl spoke so quickly that William could not completely understand what she said, he did understand *entrez*, and stepped forward, following the girl inside.

"La couverture," the little girl said. "Vous aimez?"

William pursed his lips and squinted, shrugging his shoulders. "I don't speak français."

"Papa!" the little girl shouted. "Client anglais!"

"Il est au sous-sol," a voice from the other side of the store shouted. "Il ne peut pas t'entendre."

William looked to the far corner of the shop. An older girl was seated behind a desk, a pen in one hand, a book in the other. She lowered her head slightly, peering over the rim of her glasses, and said to William, "My father's in the basement. Despite my sister's efforts, he will not hear."

She smiled, looked back down at her book, and began to write in a notebook.

The girl who invited William inside pursed her lips, stamped her feet, walked back to the far wall, pointed her finger at the girl William assumed was her older sister, and yelled, maybe threatened. She then turned, walked behind the counter, drew back a curtain with a sweep of her hand, and began running and shouting, "Papa! Papa! Client anglais! Mon client anglais!"

"Mon client anglais." William wondered if it meant what he thought it meant—that this English person who had just entered the shop was the little girl's customer, and nobody else had the right to steal the potential sale from her.

William turned and looked through the window, out into the mass of humanity celebrating. After witnessing the interaction between the two girls, he considered leaving, not wanting to be the cause of commotion. He looked back at the older girl. She had just turned a page in the book and was looking up at the ceiling, with a look of contemplation and intellectual wrestling that William understood.

William took one step toward the front door and had begun to turn when she asked, "You would like to look at the quilts up close. No?"

She placed the book on the desk and walked to the front of the store near the window display. She extended her hand. "Step closer," she invited. She looked up at the ceiling again, this time pursing her lips, and muttered, "How do you say, 'Make yourself at home' . . . yes? That is how they say in America . . . no?"

William smiled. "You know I am American?"

She giggled, then nodded.

"It's all right," William assured. "I know I don't sound like the English."

"Do not be frightened by my sister," the girl said. "Sophia is . . . how do you say? Has wild imagination? No?"

She stepped closer to the window and extended her hand. "Please," she invited.

William stepped up into the slightly elevated display and reached out to touch the quilt spread on the bed. The familiar sensation of warm tickles as he glided his palm over the fabric confirmed the composition of the quilt to be the same as the one back in New York. He ran his fingers over the white of the quilt, then felt the bulge of the brown fabric used by the creator to make the farmhouse.

He turned to examine the quilt extended between the two poles and determined that it also must have been created by the same artisan.

Footsteps approached from behind the curtain amid a barrage of shouts. "Papa! Papa! Mon! Mon!"

An arm drew back the curtain, creating a crevice through which Sophia emerged walking backward, pulling the other arm of the man who had parted the curtain.

"Mon, Papa, mon!" she insisted, still pulling, stomping her feet, and frowning at her sister and William. "Mon!"

Papa stepped from behind the curtain, leaning forward, bending low as if his daughter's determination had overpowered his strength. "Oui, chérie," he laughed, tumbling to his knees and placing his hand atop Sophia's head. "Oui."

His eyes were wide, and his smile grew as he looked at his daughter on the other side of the counter, then back at Sophia. He ruffled her hair and wrapped his long arms around her tiny body.

The older girl cleared her throat, and her father looked up as she tilted her head toward William and shifted her eyes in his direction.

The man turned, looked at William, released Sophie, and stood. By the time he raised himself from the floor, his smile had disappeared and his eyes had narrowed. He rubbed his face, looked beyond William at the celebration in the streets, and shook his head.

"What are you doing here?" he asked.

"Papa," Sophia's sister interrupted, "this is an American soldier. Sophie's customer."

Papa turned to look at his older daughter, then watched William.

"Why are you here?" he asked again. "Is anyone with you?"

William looked down at his legionnaire uniform and considered whether the family sympathized with the Germans.

"Papa!" the sister said in a tone of embarrassment. "He was looking at the quilts."

"The quilts?" Papa repeated, and he strode toward William.

His legs were long, his torso lean, his face gaunt like Abe Lincoln without the beard. After taking several strides, he stopped. He fixed his eyes on William and lowered them, making William feel like an animal in a cage being studied by a patron at the city zoo.

"My daughter says you are interested in purchasing one of the quilts."

Sophie raced forward to her father's side. "Papa . . .!"

"La patience," he said, placing his hand atop Sophie's head. "Pas maintenant."

He turned his attention back to William. "Why?" he asked. "Why the keen interest in the quilts?"

It was odd to be asked questions framed in a way that made William feel he was under suspicion for a crime, but he saw no need to conceal the truth.

"I have one at home in New York, very similar to the ones in your window."

"Katerina," the man said, pointing toward the desk where his elder daughter had been studying. "Take your sister, give her a color book . . . something, anything to do. Go downstairs and tell your mother we have a visitor."

"Yes, Papa." Katerina turned, took Sophie's hand, and walked to the back of the store.

The father looked down at William and smiled. "Sophie . . . my youngest," he explained. "By shouting louder than her ten siblings, she thinks this will help her mother and me not to forget she exists."

The man smiled, relieving the anxiety William felt building, but William shuddered to think of the chaos in this home.

"You are American?" the father asked.

"Yes, sir."

"Yet the uniform?"

"I joined the legion before our president declared war."

"Well," the father said, "whatever uniform you wear, unless it be German, you are welcome in our store."

Again, this released more tension.

"Hmm," the father continued. "Still, it is curious—your interest in the quilts."

"I meant no disrespect. It's just they are so similar . . ."

The man rubbed his face, watching William, then glanced at the window display. "Their history is dark," he explained, "and most in the city, in this area, are aware of the man who created them. That is perhaps why so few have been purchased."

"Is the man still living?" William asked. And as soon as he asked it, he regretted the question, seeing the expression of suspicion reappear on the shop owner's face.

"No," the man answered, "died twenty years ago. Spent eighty years of his life wasting away in our city's jail. His tedium prompted these, but his mastery of the art made him valuable to our city's leaders. They used him to train our troops so they could defeat their own brand of tedium biding time between battles, waiting in their camps for their encounter with destiny."

"Eighty or ninety years," the father muttered, his eyes leaving William. He reached for a chair behind him and sat. "A life of a man, most of which he spent in a cage no larger than this display, used by those in power for their own amusement, as if his life was of no value."

William did some quick calculations.

"He was born in the early 1800s?"

The father nodded. "He was captured in battle. Just a boy—deaf and dumb—the drummer boy of one of Napoleon's marshals at Waterloo."

***

"You've made a friend, Papa," Katerina said, emerging from behind the curtain with a woman William assumed must be the mother.

"Ma femme chérie," the father exclaimed, standing and extending his hands. He then turned his back to William. With his right hand he made a *V* with his index and middle finger, placed his fingers near the top of his chest, pantomimed the placement of a ring on the finger of his left hand, and last, placed his right hand flat over his chest while taking a deep sigh.

He took several brisk strides toward his wife, wrapped his arms around her, and kissed her on top of her head. "Ma chérie!"

But the mother seemed to pay no regard to her husband's adoration. As soon as she stepped from behind the curtain, she raised her right hand to cover her mouth and looked at William with horror, her eyes wide and her head moving from side to side.

A flurry of hand motions ensued from the mother as she started to breathe heavily, losing her balance and almost falling until Katerina guided her to sit in a chair that the father raced to retrieve from behind the counter.

"Katerina," the father said softly.

"Oui, Papa," she said, rushing to his side.

He whispered instructions, and his daughter quickly retrieved her sister at the back desk, grabbed her hand, then raced back toward their parents and disappeared behind the curtain.

The mother's heavy breathing settled, but the flurry of hand signings did not. It was clear to William that the mother could not hear. It was also clear that the signing utilized on the two sides of the Atlantic were not identical. Most of the signings between the father and mother he could not understand, but isolated words he could figure out, words that most people who were not deaf could be able to interpret. She pointed at the tip of her nose, cupped each hand over her ears, used each index finger to point just below each eye, and ran her thumb and index finger across her mouth. William recognized that something about his own facial features had caused the mother to react as she was.

Fifteen years earlier, when William was separated from Timmy but just before Timmy walked down that long hallway and the friends sensed they would never see one another again, each extended his right hand and made a fist with his thumb sticking out one side and the pinky sticking out from the other—the sign for *same*. They brought their fists together, declaring to one another their sameness, their friendship.

Now the mother repeatedly brought her hands together, index fingers touching. The sign, William assumed, must be equivalent to the sign he and Timmy shared at their separation.

And there was a pattern. Each time she pointed at her eyes, or ears, or nose, or mouth, she would bring her index fingers together.

William began to suspect that he resembled someone the couple knew.

The father was somber. He looked at William for just a moment, then looked down at the floor, nodding. And whenever his wife looked up again, fixated by William's face, the father would look up for a moment also, then lower his eyes back to the floor. "Remarquable," he'd mutter.

"It's not the old man," William blurted, breaking the silence. "Is it?"

"Excuse me?" the father asked quietly.

"My father?" William asked with hesitancy.

The man began to laugh. His laugh started to roll. He signed something to his wife, and her face transformed from fear to amusement.

"Your father," the owner of the store explained, "is not the old man. No. But there was another man, a younger man, who we think must have been your father. He was a friend of the old man, perhaps his only friend."

"And they met in prison?" William asked, eager to get any information they knew. He didn't care what the implications were; he had never had an opportunity like this, never imagined it possible to learn anything of his parents. What did it matter who they were or what they had done?

"Yes," the man said, apologetically. "Your father had some habits . . . He was a frequent resident of the jail, but never long term . . . But after his releases, he never failed to visit the old man weekly. Taught him to read and write. Brought him new books each week. No one else ever considered the old man worth the effort. The last ten, fifteen years of his life he read the Bible countless times, could read and write not only in French but also in English, Russian, and he even began to learn Hebrew. His favorite book was Dostoevsky's *The Idiot*. 'Imagine that,' your father once told me. 'Antwerp's village idiot who can read and write in four languages.'"

The mother began to sign, and the father waited for her to finish.

The father turned to William. "She says that 'he—your father, the man we think was your father—would bring us things to sell.' Most were useless, and those that weren't, we were suspicious of . . . worried whether he had obtained them dishonestly. So, naturally, we were hesitant to sell any in the store. But when we learned of the old man's talent with the quilts, how the king had even used him to instruct his soldiers in the craft, we began to sell them."

William looked at the shop owner to continue. "And?"

"They sold, at first. But when word spread that the old man was the artisan, the people feared that perhaps they'd catch some disease or that something from the old man's assumed immorality might infect their children."

"And my father?"

The shop owner reached behind the curtain, grabbed another chair, and set it down. "Please," he said, pointing. "Sit."

William stepped past the counter and sat in the chair.

"My father? You knew him?"

"Yes. That is why I must have appeared so suspicious. Your father was not a man you could easily trust. We understood one another. We helped him find honest work, when he was ready to work honestly, and he helped protect us from the dishonest element of our city."

"Is he alive?" William asked. "Does he live in the city?"

The shop owner looked at his wife, and the wife looked at William with the expression he suspected she used on her own children when they scraped a knee.

"Then he is dead?" William asked.

"That is correct."

"And my mother?"

"We met her several times."

The shop owner signed to his wife. And his wife signed a response. A long response.

"Your father was a handsome man. He called himself Frank, but he had different names, depending on what your relationship with him was. Different employers knew him by six or seven names. Different women knew him by five, ten, twenty names—for it seemed he had a new woman with him each time he came into the shop.

"Then one day he arrived with a young woman. Beautiful woman. Spoke no English, no French . . . no Dutch, no German. We never could figure from where she arrived. We'd never seen your father with the same woman more than three or four times, but for six months they were linked arm in arm. Until she began showing.

"That was when he disappeared. We thought he was scared and could not handle the responsibility, but he returned just weeks before you'd arrive, all excited about a new venture he'd discovered.

Wanted me to become his partner. Involved diamonds. Showed me three, but I was not interested. If they were fake, I wanted no part of his scheme. If they were real, he'd not be the sort of person who could have obtained them by honest means. So I refused.

"The next day the police found him dead, lying in bed next to the mayor's wife in the mayor's home—both of them shot through the heart.

"Several neighbors saw your mother leaving the home of the mayor that evening, but the police never found her."

Katerina stepped from behind the curtain, holding a box.

"Ici c'est, Papa," she said, handing it to her father.

Sophie trailed quietly behind Katerina, her mouth pressed shut, her gaze fixed on her shoes. With her right hand gripped tightly, she dragged a small satchel.

He removed the lid from the box and reached inside, taking out a folded quilt, then placing it on the counter. He reached inside and placed a second quilt on top of the first.

"These are yours," the shop owner said. "These belonged to your father."

William stood from the chair and reached for the top quilt, unfolding it by holding it at the top edge and letting the fabric unroll toward the floor. The scene sewn onto the white background was identical to the scenes on the two quilts in the shop's window— the farmhouse and the large field surrounded by a brick wall. But this quilt, like the one in the safe-deposit back home, had writing:

וב שמתשה וצחשה דלמה

תמאה תא סורהל ידכ ויכסבו

William recognized the lettering, the left-to-right structure of the grammar, from the days he waited outside the temple while

David, Naomi, and Mara learned Hebrew basics. The writing on the blanket back home was in Russian—apparent fruits of the old man's self-education within Antwerp's jail cell.

The father nudged the second quilt to the edge of the counter, inviting William to unfurl it as he had the other. William folded the Hebrew quilt and placed it onto the counter.

As he held the top of the second quilt, revealing the familiar scene of the farmhouse, he noticed that the lettering on this quilt was in more familiar lettering, clearly Latin based, but still not something William could understand:

> *Le guerrier le plus courageux ne le tenterait pas*
> *dans la nuit d'hiver la plus froide de l'hiver*

"The bravest warrior would not tempt it," the father interpreted.
"Tempt what?" Katerina asked.
The father walked to the blanket and held out his left hand toward the writing, as if he were a teacher inviting his students to read along:

> *The bravest warrior would not tempt it*
> *On the coldest winter's night.*

Katerina stepped close to the blanket, and after looking at the lettering for several seconds, she started to giggle. "Ahh, Papa . . . je vois!"

"It's French?" William asked.
The father nodded. "Oui."
"And the other?" William asked. "Hebrew?"
The father stepped close to William, took the French blanket from his hands, and folded it, placing it back on the counter next to the Hebrew blanket.

Then he unfolded the Hebrew blanket, handed one end of it to Katerina, and spread it out between the two of them, again using his left hand to point at the words as he said:

The arrogant king used it
and a knife to destroy truth

"We are not Jewish," the father stated, "but we have many Jewish neighbors. They translated for us."

The father folded the Hebrew quilt. "Sophie," he called out, "apporte-moi le sac, s'il te plaît."

Sophie stepped forward, holding up the satchel she had been dragging.

The father tucked the folded quilts into the satchel and handed it to William.

"These are yours," he said. "There were three of them . . . only three on which the old man stitched writing. These two remain."

"But," William replied, reaching into his pocket and removing his billfold, "I must pay—"

"No," the man said. "Non, niet, ivrit. They belong to you now."

William looked around at the family. He nodded gratitude to Katerina. He signed thank you to the mother, placing his right hand over his mouth and sweeping it toward her.

He looked down at Sophie, her head tilted downward.

William removed two francs and two dollars from his billfold. He lowered to his knees, facing Sophie, and held out the four bills. "Merci," William said.

Sophie looked up, her eyes shining, her face transformed into surprise.

"Merci, monsieur! Merci!"

***

So now he knew.

When he was six, he was separated from Timmy.

When he was nine, Sir Thomas died.

He chose to leave St. Mary's one year later.

He found work in Manhattan. He found ways to survive. He educated himself. He applied and was accepted into Harvard.

Yes, he had assistance. There were Uncle Nathan, Eli, and Mrs. Chalmers; there were Luther Taylor, Mugsy McGraw, and Matty. He found safe haven in the Newsboy homes, was greeted kindly by the city librarians, and thousands of patrons bought his papers. There were other thousands, whom he had never met, who had constructed the bridges and built the trains and laid the streets which provided the avenues by which he could succeed.

But when he was nineteen, he got himself expelled from Harvard.

When he was twenty-one, Merlin died in his arms.

One day later, he discovered what he had dreamed his entire life to know.

But what he learned, what he discovered, was not a dream.

Two weeks prior to his birth, his mother killed his father.

One or two or three days later, his mother hid herself somewhere on a ship harbored in Antwerp. And there she remained undiscovered until she decided to depart. Depart the world. Depart the son to whom she had just given birth.

So now he knew.

***

Instead of proceeding to Berlin to begin the trip he had promised Merlin, William boarded the southbound train from Antwerp, disembarked in Brussels, then headed west, planning to walk until he reached Ypres to report to his escadrille that he was still alive. Then he'd figure what to do next.

One hour west of Brussels, he arrived at a sign in the road informing him that Ypres was 110 kilometers to the west, and twenty kilometers to the south was Waterloo.

William turned south.

***

Still miles away, William saw the hill on which stood the bronze lion commemorating Wellington's victory over the French. "Irony of ironies," William whispered to himself, his heart racing as he took each step nearer to the field he had imagined from his childhood. Yet Wellington despised the monument, furious that someone, or several someones, presumed it was acceptable to destroy the sight lines of his battlefield, annihilating the historical legacy for future generations.

He would have preferred to approach from the south, as Napoleon had—to see the field of battle emerge just like the great general had seen alongside his marshals. But he was following in the steps of Wellington, looking down onto the fields on which the French Army camped.

To the left, Napoleon had set up his observation base at La Belle Alliance, a long warehouse-like structure on the edge of the road that perimetered the battlefield. William raced down the hill, the satchel with the quilts bouncing up off his torso with each stride. He tightened the strap, minimizing the bounce, and reached Napoleon's headquarters. He reached for the latch on the door and tried to turn the knob, but it wouldn't budge. He knocked, but there were no lights inside and no noise. To his left there was a tall cylinder-shaped stone monument. He walked to it and saw it was a tribute to Victor Hugo. He turned to his right, toward the fields, and imagined how much of what Hugo had written in the opening pages of his novel was true, how much was imagined. William crossed the street, tugged on the strap of the satchel, and stepped onto the field of battle, searching for the Ohain sunken road that Hugo portrayed as playing a crucial role in Wellington's victory. But there was no sunken road, no sign that there had ever been a sunken road or that the fields had ever been the scene of sharp elevation changes—just the gradual increase toward Wellington's lookout at Mont-Saint-Jean.

William turned to walk north toward Wellington's camp and stopped at the small farmhouse on his left. Recreating the map of the battle in his mind, William reckoned it was La Haye Sainte, which the French had captured by midmorning and had held onto throughout most of the day. He tried to open the front door, the side door, and the rear doors, but all were locked.

Looking to the east, he imagined the terror Napoleon and his marshals felt as they saw the cloud of black uniforms emerging from the forest in the late afternoon. Napoleon had commissioned Grouchy to intercept the Prussians—to destroy their troops, to prevent them from assisting the British—but Grouchy had failed. When the black-clad Prussians emerged from the east, the French panicked and expedited their demise.

William decided to walk up to the apex of the battlefield, Mont-Saint-Jean, and try to open the doors of the structures on the north end of the battlefield. All were shut. All were locked.

He turned and looked at Wellington's Monument, the large mound of dirt. The most distinguished image on the field was the most despised by historians and by Wellington himself. There was nobody in the vicinity; nobody seemed to appreciate the historical significance of the site. There was nobody with whom William could commiserate—no Merlin, no Sir Thomas, no one. Had everyone forgotten what had happened here? Would the horror of the last four years be forgotten just as easily?

Within minutes his excitement had dissipated, replaced with an empty, gnawing recognition that not only was humanity destined to repeat its errors, but that on a much more personal level, he was alone. There was no one that cared for him—even his unit likely thought he was dead—and like all those who had lost their lives, he was a necessary casualty in securing a peace that time would deteriorate once again.

He turned to his right, hoping the road to the west would lead him back to Ypres, back to his escadrille. Just to the south of the road were some structures, the third of the settlements in which the battle had raged: Hougoumont.

If the shop owner's story was accurate about the old man whom William's father had befriended, this was the structure in which the French drummer boy had been held captive by British forces. Before embarking on his westward trek, William walked southwest through the fields and through the gates of Hougoumont.

He walked to the chapel in the center of the grounds. Legend was that when fire broke out from the French barrage, the chapel caught fire, but miraculously, it did not engulf the wooden carving of Christ on the cross on the eastern end of the chapel. The flames engulfed Christ's toes, then stopped.

William tried to open the door of the chapel, but it was locked. He peered through the windows, but they were darkened, and though he could see the crucifix on the eastern wall, there was not sufficient illumination to conclude if the legend was true.

He lowered his head. The emptiness returned.

And then he saw it.

He had seen it earlier from afar, but it had not registered.

On the edge of Hougoumont, on the very edge of the battlefield, was an elongated brown farmhouse with a chimney at either end.

William lowered the satchel from his shoulder and bent to his knees, unclasping the buckle and taking out one of the quilts.

The old man had represented it well, capturing the relative heights and lengths of the roof and walls and windows and doors. Even the colors and contrasts of the materials he had chosen to represent the farmhouse gave it a striking resemblance to what William saw before him.

He stuffed the quilt back into the satchel, placed it over his shoulder, and searched for an entrance. When he reached for the knob of the first door, the knob turned, he heard a click, and he felt the knob release its latch, he could hardly imagine it possible, based on all the other structures he hadn't been able to enter.

He leaned inside, careful not to enter someone's residence. But the room was dark, with only the setting sun illuminating the surroundings. Whereas the room had remnants of someone once living inside these walls in relative comfort, those remnants had aged: wooden chairs that had rotted, in the center of the room a leaning table with one leg visibly shorter than the other three, broken windows, a floor that had not been swept, and shard carpets infiltrated with dirt and dead insects. There was no smell of mildew, no indication that anybody had resided within the rooms of the home for years.

William walked to one of the rotting chairs and slowly tested his weight, making sure the chair would not crumble beneath him.

"Hello," he called out. "Bonjour!" he said, more loudly.

No response.

He bent over to remove the French quilt from the satchel, recalling the words that had been translated for him: "The bravest warrior would not tempt it on the coldest winter's night."

He removed the Hebrew quilt and stared at the lettering, mumbling the translation: "The arrogant king used it and a knife to destroy truth."

He whispered by memory the words on the Russian quilt back home: "The jester's princess chose it, to manifest her spite."

He looked to the ceiling, sensing the old man was conveying a message—his way of leaving a legacy, perhaps, teaching the world a lesson he had learned. But he could not figure out what that message might be. For certain, the old man was no dummy. He may have been deaf and dumb, but like Luther Taylor, he was no dummy; he was no idiot.

"Idiot," William muttered softly after he had thought of the word some might use to describe the old man. "Idiot?"

William pressed his eyelids together, recalling the events in Dostoevsky's novel. "The favorite," the shop owner had said, "the favorite of the old man."

"The jester's princess chose it, to manifest her spite." William recited out loud, repeating it once, then twice, and when he said it the third time he lowered his eyes, looking across the floor, staring at the fireplace at the far north end of the room.

"The princess," William said as he smiled. "The jester's princess . . . the idiot's princess . . . Filippovna. Tossed the rubles into the fire, spiting them all."

He stood, unfurling the Hebrew quilt. "The arrogant king used it and a knife to destroy truth."

William's smile grew. He recalled the story, intrigued by the narrative he heard while waiting for the Chalmers children at temple. "King Jehoiachin . . . right?" he whispered. "Spiting Jeremiah. Cutting the law from the scroll, throwing each piece he cut into the fire."

He unfolded the French quilt.

"The bravest warrior would not tempt it on the coldest winter's night."

William tossed the French quilt onto the chair behind him.

He walked to the fireplace and lowered to his knees.

He removed his gun from its holster and began tapping the bricks of the fireplace until he heard one in the upper left sound hollow.

He reached up and removed it after several minutes of digging his fingernails into the crevices between the bricks.

Inside was a bronze canister adorned with a portrait of three horses galloping forward into battle. William recognized it as a powder canister, similar in size and shape to the one Professor Murchinson had in his display of Civil War artifacts, possibly used by the British to hold powder for their muskets.

William opened the top of the canister carefully, unsure how the powder might react after a hundred-year dormancy.

He wasn't sure if powder would increase in density after such a long period, maybe absorb moisture and increase its weight, for whatever the canister held inside, it did not feel light, though he had anticipated it would.

He twisted open the top and turned the opening onto his palm.

Nothing came out.

He shook it and nothing seemed to budge.

He held it out in front of his eyes, trying to use the fading light from the setting sun to get a glimpse of what was inside. A twinkle from the canister's opening winked at him.

With his pinky he pried the object free, removed it, and held it between his index finger and thumb, just as he had watched Uncle Nathan hold and examine the stones he regularly valued.

He shook the canister, and now the contents jingled.

Reaching inside, he removed a second stone, its size and likeness similar to the first and resembling the three stones he had been given back home.

Uncertain as to how many of these stones rested inside, he shook his head in amazement, chuckled, placed the one diamond back into the canister, placed the brick back into its place, and raced to the entrance of the farmhouse.

He looked to his left, to his right. Looked out toward Wellington's Monument, past La Haye Sainte, past La Belle Alliance, past the forest from which the Prussians had emerged. Nobody was in sight. Nobody cared about Waterloo. Nobody had learned its lessons. Nobody would miss the diamonds nestled in the canister William now held.

***

He purchased a first-class ticket, not because he could with his probable newfound wealth, but because he still had enough currency remaining from the sale of his second diamond from home. He had used what remained to fulfill his promise to Merlin: He had visited Berlin, Moscow, Stockholm, Warsaw, Budapest, and Rome. He had returned to Paris, traveled north to Le Havre, and boarded the next ship returning to America. Still, he had funds remaining.

The stones in the ammunition canister were weighing on his conscience. If they were not real, that would be a relief; but if they were genuine, invaluable, and priceless, would he be taking something that did not belong to him?

There was no sense in worrying about it; it could amount to nothing. He would show the stones to Uncle Nathan—well, one of the stones—and observe his reaction to learn of its value. If Uncle determined they were of value, then this could be something over which he would lose sleep. He would need to find a way to use them, despite their history, despite how he had come to possess them. Regardless of the low morals of his parents, he would use the wealth for the good of humanity, to prove that he was not of the same breed as those who brought him into the world.

What a first-class ticket promised William was not prestige. It was not luxury he craved. What he was after, what he wanted, was access to the crew of the ship, the captain and his mates. To befriend them, with hopes of gaining access to their communications room, enabling him to follow the progress of the upcoming Series between the National League champion Cincinnati Reds and the heavily favored American League champion Chicago White Sox.

He was not the only interested passenger. There were ten passengers allowed by the captain to sit around the perimeter of the room in which the telegraph operator received messages.

"Redland Field," he announced when the machine began dancing. "Rigler behind the dish. Evans, Quigley, and Nallin around the bases."

After silence of about thirty seconds, the machine began its rhythm.

"First pitch from Dutch Ruether is low and outside to Shano Collins," the operator announced. "Next pitch high. Third pitch is hit sharply over second base bag for a single."

William was torn, unsure which team he would favor. The Sox were Merlin's team, but the Reds were Matty's new team. He had taken over at the end of the '16 season, one of the worst teams in either league, and turned them into a contender. When he left for the war near the end of the '18 season, they were in fourth place with a winning record. One year later, they were competing for the world championship.

Eddie Collins followed Shano's single by grounding to the pitcher, forcing his teammate at second. Then he got thrown out at second, trying to steal. Buck Weaver flew to Edd Roush in center, ending the top half of the first.

The Reds leadoff man, Morrie Rath, let Cicotte's first pitch pass without swinging. It was called a strike by Rigler. Cicotte's next pitch was high and fast, striking Rath on his right shoulder. Daubert followed with a single. Heinie Groh knocked him in for the first run of the Series.

In the fourth, Cicotte, a ground ball inducer, was apparently not getting his pitches located where he wanted. After two outs and a man on first, Neale, Cincinnati's number seven hitter, singled; the catcher, Ivey Wingo, singled. The pitcher, Ruether, tripled, then Rath doubled, Daubert singled, and the Sox manager, Kid Nichols, pulled Cicotte in the fourth. The score was 6–1. The game ended 9–1, giving the Reds a 1–0 Series lead.

The following evening Cincinnati made two costly errors, allowing the Sox to score their only two runs of the game. But

Happy Felsch's errant throw in the fourth allowed the Reds to score three of their four runs in the game, thus giving them a 2–0 Series lead. The Sox outhit Cincinnati, 10–4, but weren't able to get the key hits. They didn't seem to have the same fight as they did two years earlier when they beat McGraw's Giants. William wondered if the players felt as he did, dismissing the value of the game they played, questioning whether their actions on the field really mattered in light of the lives that had been lost not only because of the war but also from the outbreak of influenza. Millions had died—more from the disease than in battle.

As Slim Sallee retired the Sox in the bottom of the ninth, securing the Reds' win, William rose from his seat and went out to roam the deck. He looked out into the darkness—a horizon of sky and sea indistinguishable. He felt the weight of the diamonds he kept under his shirt on a string around his neck, contemplating what he would do with them if Uncle Nathan determined their value was real. He wondered if he ought to even let Uncle know how many there were.

He returned to the communications room on Thursday and found himself cheering for the Sox when their young hurler, Dickey Kerr, pitched a three-hit shutout, beating the Reds, 3–0. The score would have been much more lopsided had it not been for odd base running occurrences in the second and third innings. Again, the Sox got plenty of hits but couldn't hit in the runners.

On Saturday, Eddie Cicotte had another forgettable outing—in particular, the top of the fifth. With one out, he fielded a grounder but threw the ball over Chick Gandil's head at first, far into the seats. Then after Greasy Neale laced a double into left field, Cicotte intercepted the throw to home, cutting it off as if to throw the man at second, but he muffed the throw, and the ball ricocheted past

Schalk. Those two runs in the fifth were the only two runs scored by either team. Despite the Reds' poor hitting and their sloppy fielding, the Sox's errors proved more costly, and their inability to hit when it mattered had them down in the Series, 3–1. It was as if neither team wanted to win.

Hod Eller was the star of game five. He struck out six consecutive Sox in the second and third innings, ending the game with nine K's and allowing only three hits. Any other year the Series would be over, but the league officials had determined a best-of-nine Series would pick up the spirit of the nation following the war and in the midst of the epidemic. William could not imagine how any baseball bug could have their spirits lifted after watching or reading about the horrible play of both teams. If this was the state of the game, if this was a picture of what the nation had become during his absence, William wondered if when he arrived in New York he ought to simply disembark the ship, walk across the pier to a ship returning to Europe, and live the rest of his days on the other side of the Atlantic.

After nine innings in game six, the score was tied at four. Shoeless Joe led off the top of the tenth with a double and scored. Dickey Kerr completed the tenth by retiring the Reds in order, securing his second win of the Series. The new life the Sox showed, coming from a 4–0 deficit, filled William with some hope, erasing the doom he felt after listening to the telegraph operator's narration the previous evenings.

The Wednesday night game was a brilliant return for Cicotte— he had his ground ball magic working. Twelve of the outs recorded were ground balls to his infielders. "Brilliant!" William whispered to himself, imagining himself on the mound conserving energy, outwitting the batters, conniving the hitters into swinging at pitches that looked juicy, but as the ball dropped further than they imagined possible, they'd punch it into the ground, creating a routine grounder. The more he listened to Cicotte's masterpiece in Cincinnati that evening, the more anxious he was to return to the mound to continue the experiments he had begun at Cambridge, wondering if he could induce professional hitters as efficiently as he had induced amateurs.

He thought of the chance encounter he had with a Red Cross driver just days before boarding the ship at Le Havre. William arrived from Rome traveling by train, but the train had malfunctioned ten miles outside of Paris. Most of the passengers waited for the next train. William decided to walk.

He hadn't walked a mile when a truck pulled beside him and the driver offered him a ride.

"Bonjour!" the driver shouted. "Entrez, monsieur."

William recalled looking inside the cabin, seeing an innocent face smiling, full of hope, full of life. After all that William had seen, after traveling by himself to all the cities on Merlin's itinerary, stepping inside the truck was an easy decision.

"Merci, but I am not French."

"You are American!" the driver shouted. "My name is Walter. I shall be your chauffeur. Where may I take you?"

"Paris," William answered.

William looked to his left. On the seat between him and Walter, papers were scattered.

"These are your drawings?" William asked, picking up one of the pages.

"You like them?" Walter asked with a proud smile.

"They have punch," William answered, "and bring me right into the scene."

William was looking at one specific drawing, similar to a political cartoon, which depicted Uncle Sam teaching a lesson to Kaiser Wilhelm in a classroom.

Below the strewn pages was a bound notebook. Curious, William picked it up and began thumbing through the pages. They were filled with images depicting animals, children, and public figures. All images were drawn with equal talent.

"Tell me," Walter encouraged, "what you are thinking. What was running through your mind just now?"

William turned his head, uncertain what he ought to say.

"I saw a look in your eyes," Walter explained. "To know what created the look on your face—that is what I want to know, so I can create the look on more faces."

William shrugged. "Adventure, maybe. Helped me forget this mess the war left behind."

"Forget?" Walter said with excitement. "Forget? Excellent!"

William remembered staring at Walter, amazed at his enthusiasm. Envious of it.

"You think me strange?" Walter had asked. "My father once told me that nothing is more important than bringing joy to another. Being an instrument that brings a smile to another's face. That is what I hope to accomplish in those drawings."

William turned another page and nodded. "Mission accomplished."

"My father told us," Walter continued, as he turned right, the Eiffel Tower now in view on the horizon, "that the days he spent constructing the fair gave him the most satisfaction he ever felt at work. Seeing the children with their parents, full of happiness, enjoying one another—he played a role in that. He played a small part in making that family happy for the day."

"The fair?" William asked. "In Chicago?"

Walter turned toward William. "That's right. In '92."

William reached into his pocket and unfolded the picture of Sir Thomas.

"What have you got there?" Walter asked.

"Someone I know," William replied, "a teacher of mine when I was a kid. He worked the fair, along with the others in this picture. Like your father, he said it was the most enjoyable work he'd ever done."

Walter stopped the car at an intersection on the outskirts of the city. He leaned over to look at the photograph.

"Hah!" Walter exclaimed. "That's my papa on the far left!"

Something wonderful happened in Chicago during the World's Fair of 1892. A wonderland was constructed in which families could disappear for a day, forget their troubles, enjoy one another. Four young men contributed to this wonderland, the four men in the picture William held. Walter's father had been the only man in the picture of whom he had no knowledge, but that had changed, and now William yearned for what the four friends accomplished, what Walter had discovered—to set his hands and heart to work on something that would bring joy to others.

For Walter, it was drawing. For the four friends in the picture, it was constructing. For Eddie Cicotte, it was making a baseball dance. And what was it for William? Did his arm hold magic also? Magic that would enthrall children and capture their imaginations?

And if not ball, then what? Could he return to school, perhaps discover something else in which to excel? Something that would benefit others?

The telegraph dancing woke William from his memory of Walter, the picture, and the World's Fair. Cicotte's brilliant pitching was supported by the offense of Shoeless Joe and Happy Felsch, each with two singles and two RBIs. The Series had tightened, the Reds holding a 4–3 lead.

But something horrible happened in Chicago on the afternoon of Thursday, October 9. The telegraph operator narrated the Reds' pounding of Lefty Williams's pitches during the opening inning of game eight. Five hits later the Reds were leading, 4–0. They scored a fifth run in the second, another in the fifth, three more in the sixth, and their tenth run in the eighth. They defeated the Sox, 10–5, winning the Series, 5–3.

As New York Harbor came into view the next morning, William placed his hand over his chest, feeling the bulge of the bronze ammunition canister.

Uncertain of the diamonds' value, he feared what might happen if he were found guilty of bringing contraband back from the war.

Uncertain of his ability and prowess as a pitcher, he feared that whatever efforts he made as a professional ballplayer would end in failure.

He was certain of one thing: his ability to survive. Alone.

His separation from Timmy was an introduction. The death of Sir Thomas was confirmation. His departure from St. Mary's was proof. Merlin's death was a reminder that those closest to him would leave.

If he were to accomplish something of significance, if he were to bring smiles to the faces of others, he'd have to find the way on his own.

For Further Reading

Game events described in the narrative are based on the summaries and box scores from accounts appearing in the main editions of the following newspapers:

The Boston Globe (October 13, 1914; October 12–13, 1915; April 11, 1916; October 8 and 10–13, 1916)

Brooklyn Eagle (October 11, 1916)

Chicago Tribune (October 7–8, 11–12, 14, and 16, 1917; September 6–8 and 10–12, 1918; October 2–5 and 7–10, 1919)

New York Post (October 10, 1916)

The New York Times (October 11, 1916)

The Philadelphia Inquirer (October 10–13, 1914; October 9, 10, and 14, 1915)

The years leading to the United States' entry into the war were marked with an often antagonistic give-and-take between baseball executives and America's elected officials. Two books written by Jim Leeke—*From the Dugouts to the Trenches* and *The Gas and Flame Men*—offer perspectives of this conflict and also highlight heroic contributions made overseas by several major leaguers. Ty Cobb's recollection of events occurring at Hanlon Field in France can be found in Tim Hornbaker's *War on the Basepaths*, Charles Leerhsen's

Ty Cobb—A Terrible Beauty, and Al Stump's *Ty Cobb—My Life in Baseball*.

John Keegan's *The First World War* offers a thorough analysis of events leading up to the war as well as brief summaries of the war's many theaters. James Carl Nelson's *Five Lieutenants* explores the war's impact on five Harvard graduates and their bravery. Ring Lardner's correspondence is cataloged and edited by Jeff Silverman in *Lardner on War*. Ron Rapoport's *The Lost Journalism of Ring Lardner* contains many of Lardner's writings. The experience of Walt Disney at the end of the conflict in Europe is described in Bob Thomas's *Walt Disney: An American Original*.

Description of the Waterloo battlefield can be found in Andrew Roberts's *Waterloo* and Frank McLynn's *Napoleon* as well as in the opening chapters of Victor Hugo's *Les Misérables*.

A taste of myth, legend, and history surrounding Napoleon's fascination with diamonds can be found by googling Dragana Jovanovic's article, "Napoleon and Josephine's Engagement Ring Auction," or by googling Napoleon diamond necklace or Regent diamond.

A more in-depth analysis of the baseball events described in the narrative can be found in Bob Gaines's *Christy Mathewson*, Frank Deford's *The Old Ball Game*, John McGraw's *My Thirty Years in Baseball*, Christy Mathewson's *Pitching in a Pinch*, and Lawrence Ritter's *Glory of Their Times*.

Acknowledgments

Karen Cleghorn has once again helped produce a cleaner and more engaging narrative. Her talents and insights as an editor are invaluable.

Thank you to Sally Hanan and her team at Inksnatcher for assisting with cover design and typesetting.

I am grateful to Liam Hartley, Etienne Ceogaert, and their team at Société de Guides in Waterloo for their hospitality and guided tours as well as Antwerp by Bike for their unique style of education, leading their guests through the streets of their city.

Newspapers.com provided complete access to the original descriptions of game events. I am grateful to them and the many faithful and diligent sportswriters through the years.